HORSE COUNTRY

Friends Like These

Also by Yamile Saied Méndez

The Horse Country Series

#1: *Can't Be Tamed*

#2: *Friends Like These*

#3: *Where There's Smoke*

Blizzard Besties

Random Acts of Kittens

Wish Upon a Stray

On These Magic Shores

Shaking Up the House

HORSE COUNTRY

BOOK 2
Friends Like These

Yamile Saied Méndez

Scholastic Inc.

ISBN 978-1-338-74948-9

10 9 8 7 6 5 4 3 2 1   22 23 24 25 26

Printed in the U.S.A.   40
First printing 2022

Book design by Stephanie Yang

For Los Tres Amigos:

Valentino Méndez, Liv Reynolds,

and Navy Goeckeritz

1

Music to Her Ears

Carolina Aguasvivas loved the clip-clopping sound of dancing hoofbeats. It was her favorite music ever. But today, as she warmed up Shadow to get ready to ride, the tall gray horse's canter was a little off. The rhythm of his footfalls *sounded* okay, and he looked just fine as he circled Carolina at the end of a long lunge line, but his gait *felt* unbalanced. She didn't know how to explain it, and she didn't know what the matter was, but she loved a challenge. She was going to fix whatever was troubling him.

On any given day, a mixture of rock en español, country, reggaeton, and K-pop rang from the newly installed speakers in the large indoor arena. But today, Carolina had to fully concentrate to work with the spirited, hardheaded Arabian horse, *el cabeza dura*, as she secretly called Shadow. She'd turned the music off.

"That's good, Shadow," she said.

The horse eased into a walk after a sequence of canter-trot-canters that left them both sweaty.

Rotating slowly in the middle of the arena, Carolina closed her eyes and followed the lead rope's progression and the rhythm of Shadow's feet as he walked around her. She wanted to get the warm-up done so Kimber, the main trainer and head of the newly established Unbridled Dreams program, would let her get on the saddle already.

If only Shadow would give her a chance. If only Kimber didn't insist on her students nailing the groundwork before she allowed any actual riding.

A little boy laughed and broke Carolina's concentration. And Shadow's. His steps faltered, like a record scratch.

Carolina sighed and opened her eyes.

A small audience had gathered to watch the training session: Chelsie Sánchez (Carolina's friend and the daughter of

Paradise Ranch's owner, Heather Whitby) and the Sullivan siblings, Bracken and Loretta.

The little gap-toothed boy was Carolina's reading buddy at school. Bracken took any chance he could to come to Paradise and read to the horses. Reading hadn't been his favorite before, but he'd do anything for time at the barn, even extra homework. He adored Carolina and was cheering for her.

Loretta was another story.

She stood by the door of the arena, looking at her phone. Caro was sure her nemesis was watching for a mistake so she could gloat that she was the best rider in the sixth grade.

Carolina tried to ignore her.

She had always wished for the place to be bursting with people and activities. She wouldn't go back to the lonely days of the past when she'd been the only kid at the ranch. But sometimes Caro missed being able to do as she wanted, or to fail without any witnesses around. It wasn't like she could kick Loretta out of the arena though.

Unbridled Dreams, the new riding and sponsorship

program at Paradise Ranch, had welcomed a few weekly students already. Carolina was painfully aware that if they wanted to extend the benefits of working with horses to kids who couldn't afford the lessons, then they couldn't lose any of the paying students. And Loretta was very much one of them.

The new riding program had been Carolina's and Chelsie's idea last year after they'd messed up grandly, trying to train Chelsie's new horse, Velvet, on their own. Though the two girls hadn't exactly hit it off right away, they *had* made some of the same rash decisions.

Creating this program to give back to the community was the way Chelsie and Carolina were making up for their mistakes. They both knew access to horses was both fun and *rewarding*, as Caro's mom always put it. But anything to do with them was very expensive, so Carolina and Chelsie had insisted on a sponsorship component.

That's why the program couldn't fail.

And so Carolina couldn't tell Loretta off. Anyway, she had other things to worry about. She couldn't let her guard down with Shadow. Today, he was giving her a harder time than usual.

The dappled gray Arabian was one of the most handsome horses at Paradise Ranch. Velvet, Chelsie's bay Thoroughbred, was gorgeous, and she'd always have a special place in Carolina's heart. But Shadow needed to stay busy or he became cranky.

Kimber had suggested Carolina take a lesson with him.

"Shadow has a . . . How can I say it?" Kimber had said. "A special temperament. You'll enjoy him."

Special temperament was code for opinionated and stubborn, which fit Carolina's description too. But Shadow and Chelsie got along grandly. Carolina had taken the challenge.

Now here she was.

Outside, a typical Idaho winter storm raged. But inside the arena, the temperature was high. The clash of their tempers— the horse's and the girl's—showed up from the start when Shadow reluctantly did the warm-up grounding exercises. Now, he absolutely refused to join up.

The join-up was that moment when rider and horse met in the middle, literally. The horse would step toward the rider, human and animal bonding before a riding session, once their trust in each other was established.

Carolina went through every action of the process precisely.

She was firm and direct in her commands. Although at eleven she was tiny next to the majestic horse, he needed to know she was in charge.

Shadow didn't want to accept her authority though. If only he weren't so stubborn, Carolina knew he'd enjoy their lesson too.

"Come here, Shadow." Carolina made kissing sounds to encourage him to walk up to her, but he stood at the far end of her lead near the wall and wouldn't budge.

"Let's try something different," Kimber intervened, jumping into the arena.

Carolina doubted the trainer could get him to cooperate, but she had to swallow the words. In less than a minute, Kimber had him loping around in circles, all obedient and compliant.

Irritated, Carolina tried not to roll her eyes, but prickly heat rose all the way to the tips of her ears.

"Let me try," she said, taking the lead rope from the trainer's hands.

She mimicked all of Kimber's movements and actions, like a dance she'd learned by heart.

But nothing worked. She avoided looking directly into his eyes. She tried to control her breath, and still the big stubborn Shadow remained in his spot.

"Take a step toward him," Kimber suggested from the edge of the arena.

"You can do it, Caro!" Chelsie cheered from the stands.

Carolina briefly glanced in the direction of her friend and sent her a thumbs-up. She appreciated the confidence shining in Chelsie's hazel eyes, but she wasn't going to budge.

Her favorite instructor on YouTube, Tina Hodges, suggested not to take that first step toward the horse and not to give in.

"Just a little step, Caro," Kimber urged. "Just try it."

Carolina hesitated, torn between the trainer she'd admired online and the one right in front of her, the one who was everything she one day hoped to become.

Finally, grudgingly, she stepped toward Shadow.

He took two steps back.

Carolina snorted, sounding like a horse.

Bracken laughed, but Chelsie leaned over to him. He placed a hand over his mouth. Even across the distance, Carolina saw the corners of his eyes were still crinkly with amusement.

Carolina was not amused.

"Give him a few seconds," Kimber instructed, sounding hopeful.

Carolina sighed. She had taught herself all she knew about horses, with the occasional guidance from her dad or Tyler, one of the former ranch hands. But her dad had been too busy managing the ranch, and Tyler had left for college just a few months ago. She'd watched videos online, but she had craved having an instructor in real life.

Now here was Kimber, and Carolina was having a hard time following her instructions.

She took another step toward Shadow. The horse snorted loudly, but to her surprise and delight, this time he didn't step back. Instead, he started walking toward her. But his attitude! He shook his mane as if to say he was doing her a favor.

Her feathers got ruffled. But fighting the urge to snap at him, she waited.

When he finally reached her, Bracken clapped, and Chelsie shushed him. "Don't distract them."

"Took you long enough," Carolina said, trying to pat Shadow's head.

The horse moved out of the way, refusing her love.

Carolina knew she shouldn't take things personally, but she was a little hurt the horse wouldn't love her unconditionally like all the other animals in the barn, including Velvet, did.

She tried to push her wounded ego aside and swung herself up in the saddle without having to use the mounting block.

"Nice!" Bracken said.

From the corner of her eye, she saw Loretta had put her phone down and was watching her every move.

Cheeks burning, Carolina kept her shoulders squared, head held high, hands soft on the reins. Shadow started walking and then swiftly transitioned to a trot.

One two, one two, she chanted along with his rhythm in her mind as Shadow started moving around the arena. Still, she felt his pent-up desire to break into a run. Carolina wanted to do everything perfectly for her audience.

Loretta had switched from her trainer from Boise to Kimber just a couple of weeks ago. She'd had the honor of becoming the first official Unbridled Dreams student besides Chelsie, whose mom owned the property, and Carolina, whose dad was the general manager. They weren't supposed to compete against each other—at least not officially—but secretly, Carolina wanted to be the best equestrian at Paradise. After all, she was the one who'd lived on the property her whole life.

Loretta watched intently, her face inexpressive.

Carolina didn't trust her. Loretta had been complying with the new rules Ms. Whitby had imposed, like how every rider had to know how to muck a stall and take care of horses if they wanted to take lessons. Loretta, who'd always looked down her nose at barn chores, did as she was supposed to. Carolina hadn't heard her complain. Yet. But she knew sooner or later, Loretta would try to find a way to get out of doing chores.

"Keep your mind on the saddle," Kimber called out.

Shadow's trotting had slowed down to a lazy walk.

"Use your aids," Kimber reminded her.

"Let's go, Shadow." Carolina pressed her outside leg against his girth. He was a big animal, but he should obey her prompt to speed up. He always obeyed Chelsie. Besides, he liked running fast without a rider on his back. Carolina had seen him racing Velvet in the paddock as if they were playing a game.

But he definitely had a mind of his own.

He didn't obey the first command, so Carolina insisted.

He remained stubbornly walking.

"Use your weight," Chelsie called at her.

Ay! Things must have been looking sad for Chelsie to chime in when she'd scolded Bracken for distracting Carolina before.

Carolina sat deeper in the saddle, using her weight as her friend had suggested.

Nothing.

She made kissing sounds and shook the reins.

Still, he walked.

Loretta chuckled.

Carolina glanced quickly in her direction.

In that moment, Shadow took off. But it wasn't the trot Carolina was expecting. It was a full-on gallop.

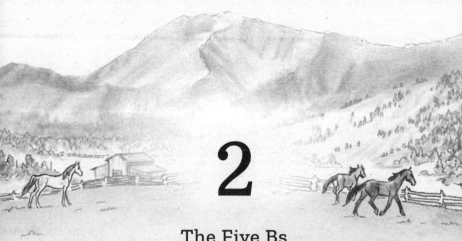

2

The Five Bs

Shadow went from snail's pace to thunderbolt in three seconds.

Carolina wasn't ready, but she was an adept rider. She sat back and gently used her seat and legs to ask him for a halt.

Instead, Shadow picked up his pace. Although she knew to push her boots in the stirrups and sway her hips to the rhythm of his pace, instinctively, she pulled her knees up instead.

There's a time and place for pulled-up knees, like on an English saddle in a show. But this wasn't the time or the place. And this wasn't the right audience for Carolina and Shadow not to get along. But she couldn't help it. She didn't trust him. And sadly, he didn't trust her. But why?

"Whoa," she called loudly, her voice shaky with fear as she pulled the reins back.

He didn't slow down.

Carolina imagined he was smiling, the rascal, and her armpits prickled with nerves.

From the corner of her eye, she saw Kimber jump into the ring. The trainer's dark, shiny braid swung over her shoulder like a lasso. Her hair contrasted against the bright pink of her shirt and the lovely umber of her skin.

At the sight of her, Shadow slowed right down and lowered his head in submission, the perfect picture of obedience.

What did I do? his attitude said.

The big stinker!

Loretta was texting furiously, a smirk on her face.

Bracken looked worried, his hands clasped like he'd been saying a prayer for Caro's safety. Chelsie was talking to him gently. How were he and Loretta related?

Carolina tried to calm her ragged breath, but the shot of adrenaline from attempting to keep up with spirited Shadow still had her heart galloping out of control.

Seeing the somber expression that clouded Kimber's face didn't help her heart rate slow down at all. The trainer's lips were pressed in a line that Carolina's mind filled with words of disappointment. But when Kimber turned to the horse, her face softened as she patted Shadow's back. He didn't deserve affection after having betrayed his rider!

"I don't know why he won't listen to me."

"I'm sure he's wondering the same thing," Kimber said, smiling up at Carolina.

Carolina's temper jumped like the spout of a hot spring. "What? Me? I was listening to him the whole time. He just won't budge."

"Didn't you hear his canter was off balance even before you got in the saddle?"

Carolina set her jaw. She *had* heard that. Why hadn't she gone with her hunch?

Kimber continued giving her advice. "Also, remember not to pull so hard at the reins. It hurts his mouth." She carefully took the reins from Carolina's hands. "And heels down." Raised knees never made it past Kimber's notice.

Carolina sighed, disappointed that she hadn't done things perfectly. Her expectations were always so high.

"I know about the reins," she said, dismounting in a smooth move she'd practiced obsessively . . . on Pepino, who was the mellowest pony in the world.

She landed heavily; Shadow was a lot taller than old Pepino. But she kept her feet. At least she had that going for her.

"Why does he listen to Chelsie and not me?"

"The thing is, you're telling him two things at once," Kimber said, answering Carolina's question while keeping comparisons with Chelsie out of her mouth. "Your words say to go, but your body says to halt. He doesn't know which command to obey."

Carolina was seething with frustration.

"Why do you look disappointed?" Bracken asked, blurting out the truth as always. "At least you didn't fall when he wouldn't stop."

"It's just that . . ." Carolina sighed again. "I don't know why my mind is blank when he does the opposite of what I was expecting."

"You and Shadow are the same," Bracken said.

"What do you mean?"

His cheeks were cherry red. "You both want to do things your own way. Remember the first *Be* of Unbridled Dreams: *Be the leader your horse needs.*" Bracken's voice got high pitched as he pointed his index finger.

He wasn't part of Unbridled Dreams yet—he could join once he turned ten, in three years. But a couple of hours after Chelsie had tacked the poster on the bulletin board, he'd already memorized the program's goals, the Five Bs. When it was his turn to go through the program, he'd know more than anyone else. It had taken Carolina a little longer than a few hours, but she could recite the whole thing now too.

1. Be the boss.

    Be the leader your horse needs.

2. Be a good teammate.

    Many hands make the work light.

3. Be focused.

    Goals lead to results.

4. Be responsible.

Your horse depends on you to make good choices.

5. Be present.

When you're in your saddle and breathe deeply, you will connect with everyone and everything around you.

Kimber had carefully constructed the principles that each of the program's students would (hopefully) learn during their lessons at Unbridled Dreams.

Carolina wanted to believe she already knew all the lessons. Apparently, she still had a long way to go if she wasn't past the first principle.

"How am I giving him mixed messages, Kimber?" she asked. As she'd recently learned with Chelsie, she couldn't do things on her own. For the best results, she needed help, and Kimber was right there, ready to offer her expertise.

"You're holding your breath, and that makes you tense."

"But you said to keep my core strong," Carolina countered.

Kimber ruffled her hair. "Tense and strong aren't the same thing, girlie."

Carolina realized she was holding her breath even now, and she exhaled, letting her shoulders fall.

"How do I do that?"

"Try to exhale slowly, in a controlled manner, when his pace changes to a fast trot so you're ready to go when he decides to bolt in a gallop," Kimber said. She made it sound so easy.

Carolina shook her head. "But I don't want him to bolt into a gallop without my instructions. He does it on purpose. He's not going to win," Carolina said, knowing she sounded as stubborn as Shadow acted.

Bracken shrugged. "I thought he was smiling when he was galloping. He loves it."

"Exactly," Kimber said. "He knows you're getting annoyed at him but you're insecure as to who the boss is. Remember principle number one."

"Be a boss," Bracken recited.

He was so annoying and adorable at the same time.

Chelsie was pointing at the big clock by the door. It marked the top of the hour.

Loretta walked into the arena like she owned the place. "Let's get you cleaned up, Shadow!"

Carolina had to bite her lip so she wouldn't say anything rude to her.

Usually after a lesson, Carolina would cool down the horse. In the summer she'd give him a good shower with the hose. But late Decembers in Idaho are extra cold, and besides, Kimber wanted to expose Shadow to as many riders and caretakers as possible to prepare him for lessons. Today's chore of getting him bedded was Loretta's.

Carolina hated to hand him to her archnemesis, but she had important Unbridled Dreams business to attend to.

"He's all yours," Carolina said.

"You're my favorite, Shadow!" Loretta said in the most irritating voice in the world.

More irritating was the horse. He nickered lovingly at Loretta and followed her to the big barn for his beautifying session.

So far, he got along wonderfully with everyone. Everyone except Caro.

Chelsie bounded up to her with a huge smile on her face. "Don't be too hard on yourself. Ready to choose our first lucky person?"

It was hard not to smile when she saw how excited Chelsie was.

There had been a slush of applications for the one twelve-week scholarship spot they had. Today, they would choose the lucky person.

Carolina wanted *everyone* to have a chance to learn from the horses, but so far, their program only had the funds to sponsor one new student. An outdoor outfitter also named Paradise, after their town, had paid for all the expenses. According to Heather, who'd become friends with the store owners, they'd be willing to sponsor more children if the feedback from the first student was stellar.

Heather had reminded the girls that next fall they'd assess if the scholarships could continue. Carolina wanted to make sure the first person set the perfect path to total success for the kids who'd come later on.

She walked away with Chelsie, following Kimber and

Bracken. He chattered like a chipmunk, and the trainer ruffled his hair. Carolina turned around just in time to see Shadow and Loretta walking cozily together. Shadow swished his tail as though just for Carolina.

Chelsie draped an arm over her shoulder. "Don't mind him, Caro."

"Easy for you to say," Carolina whispered with jealousy. "You have Velvet, your heart horse. Shadow hates me!"

A heart horse was something Carolina had wanted all her life. Some days, it seemed like she'd never find her one true horsey love.

"He'll come around; you'll see. And I'm sure the first sponsored student will just adore you. Like everyone else!"

Carolina smiled.

Finally, they would choose the first student to join their program, and whoever it was, they would become her friend. She just knew it.

3

Lucky First

Carolina couldn't shake off the drama from the arena, but for now, she had to shove it to the back of her mind. She took her boots off in the mudroom of the mansion house, as she still called Ms. Whitby and Chelsie's home. She shook the snow and dust from her jacket, imagining she was shaking her frustrations away.

The trick worked, or maybe it was just that even from the door, she could hear the fire crackling happily in the living room.

Kimber, Chelsie, and Bracken spilled into the house behind Caro.

"It smells delicious!" Kimber said, taking her boots and

jacket off and putting them in the crate and on the hook where they belonged.

"That'd be Heather's cookies." Carolina could almost taste Ms. Whitby's gooey chocolaty confections. "She promised Chelsie she'd make some for our meeting."

"I thought she was busy with the remodel," Kimber said.

"She always makes time for us," replied Carolina.

"Wow." The trainer blinked as if she couldn't believe her eyes. "It looks amazing!"

Carolina felt the same awe each time she walked into the mansion. Under Heather's supervision, a tireless crew of builders and designers had completely renovated every room. The changes were amazing.

When Carolina was little, the big house had felt almost like a museum. Mrs. Parry's dolls displayed in glass-front cabinets had been terrifying. Their vacant expressions still gave her the creeps.

Back in those days, the great room had been dark and stuffy, with wood paneling on the walls and ceiling and heavy drapes that hid the majestic views out the windows.

Now, even though it was nearly dark outside, the curtains were wide open, and the view of the valley was breathtaking. The White Cloud Mountains wore their winter robes of pristine snow and evergreens.

Inside, the great-room lights were bright and warm. The sleek couches and chairs almost looked too clean to sit in, but the Christmas decorations were cheery and inviting.

Caught in the remodeling frenzy, Heather had suggested they also renovate the cottage at the top of the hill where Caro and her parents lived. Carolina's parents had been grateful, but they asked to push it off till the spring or summer, which Carolina assumed was code for "never." Caro wouldn't say no to heated bathroom floors, but deep in her heart, she was hesitant to change anything about their little cottage. She loved the coziness of her home, even though she also loved the stark beauty of Heather's minimalistic style.

"Come on over," Heather called from the kitchen table, the only messy spot in the house.

Carolina's mom was going through a stack of papers beside her. "Hi, girls! How was training?"

Carolina kissed her mom on the cheek and rolled her eyes. "It was okay."

"Not that good, huh?" Heather guessed, tying a pink ribbon around a wrapped package.

Carolina hated to admit that classes were harder than she had expected. She was used to teaching herself haphazardly, a little thing here, another there. She wanted to impress Heather, who had always complimented her riding. Admitting things weren't perfect was hard.

"Let's just say we all witnessed one of the greatest tugs-of-war between a girl and a horse ever," Chelsie said, taking a bite out of a cookie. She chewed and winked at Carolina. Chelsie was joking, but the comment jabbed at Caro's ego.

"And who won in your opinion?" Carolina's mom asked.

"Obviously the horse," Bracken exclaimed. He sat next to Chelsie and grabbed a cookie.

"And how did you reach that conclusion?" Carolina asked, hands on her hips, but she felt the corner of her mouth tug up at the chocolate already smudged all over his face.

Bracken pressed himself against Chelsie, smearing her

favorite pink hoodie with chocolate too. "He got under your skin . . . That's why he won even though you got him to do what you wanted."

"A-ha!" Heather said. "It seems our little hardheaded Caro has met her match."

They all laughed—even Carolina, grudgingly.

She grabbed a cookie too. The chocolate melting on her tongue improved her mood like magic. "Okay, stop laughing at me! We have important work to do."

"So do we," Heather said, heading to the door where Caro's mom was already waiting.

Carolina's heart fell. "You're leaving?"

"I'm heading to the library to deliver bookmarks and flyers." Her mom clutched a manila envelope close to her chest.

"And I have a meeting with the sponsor to finish up the details," Heather said.

Chelsie and Carolina exchanged an excited look.

"Text me the name of the person you end up choosing so I can share it with them. Okay?" Heather said.

"Me too!" said Caro's mom. "I'll make a name tag and personalize the journal while I'm in town."

At that cue, Bracken said, "Here you go, Mrs. Aguasvivas," handing her one of the goodie bags filled with treasure.

Carolina and Chelsie exchanged another look—this one of amusement at how he always tried to get Caro's mom's name right, although it was a mouthful for him.

The moms smiled and headed out.

Faces glowing with excitement, Carolina, Chelsie, and Bracken gathered around the table by the fireplace while Kimber looked on.

"I wish we could choose everyone," Chelsie said longingly. Like Carolina, this wasn't the first time she made this argument.

"Me too," said Kimber. "But Caro's mom was clear. We can't afford more than one scholarship student at a time." Jen Aguasvivas was the ranch's accountant and she kept track of all the expenses. "We can't get carried away."

Carolina sighed. "I too wish we could help everyone at once, but I get why we have to go slowly."

"Why?" Bracken asked, frustrated.

"Well," Carolina said, shrugging. "Like my mom and Heather said, if we do one scholarship at a time, we can iron out the wrinkles that pop up. You don't know what you don't know, and there might be things we want to adjust after the first student's feedback."

Kimber nodded. "That's why the journal idea was brilliant," she said, grabbing one from the pile on the table. Chelsie, Carolina, and Kimber had designed all the stationery for Unbridled Dreams, the program goals, and the vision statement.

The five guiding principles of the program were printed on the inside of the journals as well as on bookmarks that they'd donated to the libraries at school and in town to create more buzz. Mr. Eves, the bookmobile librarian and driver, kept a whole stack to give away to the customers who lived far from Paradise.

The journal also had a section of tear-out pages for the students to write suggestions or feedback. Kimber had bought a clear box online that she had placed in the little barn's newly renovated hangout room for all to see.

If Shadow wrote a review on Carolina, what would he say? Carolina shuddered a little at the thought.

Chelsie pulled the stack of folders closer to her, and Carolina's excitement grew. Whose name would they print out in a special label to put over the last cubby in the little barn?

The applications were anonymous. Only Kimber knew the applicants' gender, age, and other identifying personal details, and she and Ms. Whitby had whittled down the stack to some finalists already. Carolina, Chelsie, and Bracken took turns rereading the final five applications aloud. But when Bracken got tired (he'd already met his quota reading to Twinkletoes and Bella, the ranch's mini donkey and horse, in the little barn), Kimber took over.

Carolina listened to her trainer attentively. People were so complex! Some applicants had lived in the area a long time and had always wanted to try the classes at Paradise when the old clinic was still functioning, but they hadn't dared to because none of their friends wanted to join. Or they'd been scared to try something new because of the commitment.

As the horse girl in Paradise who didn't ride to compete,

unlike Loretta and Tessa, Carolina had been lonely sometimes. How many friends she could have had if people hadn't minded what others would think!

But still, the most common reason for not taking lessons, time and again, was how expensive they were.

"See?" Chelsie said. "Our community needs Unbridled Dreams."

When Kimber was done reading the last application, there was a brief pause.

"What do you think?" Carolina asked.

"Let's read the last application again," Chelsie said.

Carolina cleared her throat and read:

"'I'm hardworking, responsible, and motivated.'" Her spine started tingling. "'In Florida, I volunteered at the animal shelter, but we had to move again, the second time in three years. When I saw the flyer for Unbridled Dreams, I thought it would be the best way for me to adjust to Paradise, become part of the community even if I might only stay in the area for a short time. Some of the other riding programs I looked at focused on competitions, but I'm more interested in learning leadership skills.'"

"The first B!" Bracken said, again with the pointed index finger.

There was a moment of silence as they all considered.

"Well . . ." Carolina said. "I think it's obvious, don't you? Especially if this is the first chance they'll have to work with horses, we can make sure it's the best experience of their lives."

All around, every head nodded in affirmation.

"Now, let's see who this person is," Kimber said, her smile blazing.

Finally. The moment they had all been waiting for.

Carolina wanted to rip open the envelope and find out right that second, but she was determined to be more of a team player. She glanced at Chelsie.

"Together?"

A smile on her face, Chelsie was already by her side. Across the table from them, Bracken's cheeks were flushed with excitement, his eyes sparkling like disco lights.

Chelsie opened the envelope, and both girls read in unison, "Gisella Bassi, ten years old, she/her, first language: Spanish."

They all cheered.

Bracken was the loudest. "How lucky!"

Inside the envelope, there was a picture of a girl. Carolina studied it intently. The girl had sad, piercing greenish eyes and a stubborn set to her jaw that made her instantly likeable. She looked younger than ten, with two long braids framing her heart-shaped face. Her hair was bay, Carolina thought at first, the same color as Velvet's coat. But then she corrected herself, laughing; it was auburn.

Her skin was fair, with freckles dotting the girl's upturned nose and round cheeks. She looked like someone who liked to spend time outdoors but had been stuck inside for too long.

Chelsie grabbed the picture and studied it for a second before she gasped.

"What?" asked Carolina.

"I know this girl!"

"Me too," Bracken said, narrowing his eyes as if that helped him recognize the girl better.

Carolina scratched her head. "She looks familiar . . ."

"Of course! You know her too, Caro," Chelsie said. "We met her right before winter break."

Carolina racked her brain, but she couldn't place her.

Chelsie huffed impatiently. "You heard her say Feliz Navidad to the EL teacher. You said that for an Idaho girl she had a perfect accent, and she said she was from Venezuela. Remember?"

The brief exchange sparked to life in Carolina's mind. She remembered it vividly now, down to the scent of gingerbread and cinnamon coming from the classroom. She had thought the girl's accent was better than hers and, honestly, had felt a stab of jealousy. To Carolina's credit, as she was riding home that day, she'd planned on talking to Gisella once school resumed. But with the break, and preparations for the holidays and the program, she'd completely forgotten there was another Latina at school. That day, she'd never even introduced herself, and now she regretted it.

"You two went off about Velvet Lilly," Carolina said, who at the time had been preoccupied with making sure the EL teacher gave out the Unbridled Dreams flyers to all her students.

Chelsie nodded, fidgeting with her Velvet Lilly charm necklace. She'd bought it at the K-pop band's last concert in San Francisco last year. "The Velveteen Army is a real thing!"

"She's very nice," Bracken said. "She's kind of quiet, and I thought she was just shy. But maybe she doesn't speak a lot of English? I didn't know she was Spanish." He tapped his chin with a pen that had a horse with a plume in its bridle at the end. Carolina's mom had found them in one of those teacher's supplies bulk stores.

"She's not Spanish," Chelsie lovingly corrected him. "She *speaks* Spanish but it says here she's from Venezuela."

"I had no idea Latina people had green eyes!" he exclaimed.

"That goes to show," Kimber said, "don't judge a Latina by her cover."

Like Carolina and Chelsie, Kimber was a Latina—an Afro-Latina whose family was from the Dominican Republic. Carolina understood Bracken's confusion. On Papi's side of her family, skin colors ranged from very pale to dark bronze, and they were all related.

Carolina felt terrible that last semester she'd been so obsessed with saving Velvet and proving her own place at the farm that she hadn't been her normal self at school, making sure everyone was included. She knew what it was like to be left out.

"What do you know about her, Bracken?" Kimber asked, looking at the photo. "Is she in your grade?"

"She's actually in fourth grade, two grades above me. Like I said, she's nice, and she loves dogs." Bracken was already the expert in all things Gisella, it seemed.

"We're going to make her feel at home and welcomed and loved and cherished," Chelsie said, glancing at Carolina. "From her letter, it seems like she'll be an easy student to mentor. She wants to be a leader and she has experience with animals."

"As co-counselors in training, I know you two will be great mentors for her," Kimber said. "But most importantly, I hope you will both become great friends with Gisella. The human aspect will make Unbridled Dreams stand out against other programs. Counselors, volunteers, and horses will shape the students' experience at Paradise. We all have a role to fulfill. Remember principle number two."

"Be a good teammate. Many hands make the world light," Bracken recited.

"Work, Bracken," Carolina said. "Many hands make the work light."

"And what did I say?" Bracken asked, perplexed.

But Carolina was already lost in her own thoughts. She had very specific ideas on how to teach riding to a person who'd never had any experiences with horses. Ideas that were very different from Chelsie's.

She loved her friend. But she wondered which one of their teaching and riding styles would be better for their first student.

Before her ideas flew away, she grabbed a napkin and jotted down the most important thing she wanted Gisella to learn: to trust herself. To do that, she'd have to have the right tools of horseback riding.

Gisella's experience had to be the best, not only so she'd write a good review for the sponsor, but because Carolina wanted her to fall in love with horses. Even horses that gave her a hard time, like Shadow.

Carolina's brain was whirring with ideas.

Next week couldn't come fast enough.

4

Out of the Loop

Carolina hummed the chorus of "Crystal Blossom," the catchiest Velvet Lilly song she'd found, as she ran to the big barn for Gisella's welcome. The day was glorious. The temperature had dipped below freezing, but the sky was a bright blue. The gravel glittered like diamonds and crunched under her boots.

She was running late, like always. But in her defense, she'd wanted to make sure the little barn and the lesson horses were ready to make the best first impression ever. Chelsie had assured her everything was flawless already, but Carolina couldn't help but double-check.

Although she had already looked through Gisella's welcome goody bag, she went through it again. Everything in the canvas tote was perfect—from the journal to pens and pencils, and a couple of stickers with the logo that featured Twinkletoes and Velvet.

The journal was a custom-made spiral notebook, divided into five sections for the students to keep track of their progress through the Five Bs during their lessons.

Since the day they'd all chosen Gisella, Carolina had been collecting ideas for today's class on a napkin, and then she'd transferred them to her own journal. But the journal was a little bulky, so she'd ripped out the page and put it in her pocket to have it handy for today. Bright-eyed and bushy-tailed, she walked into the crowded office in the big barn just as Kimber was speaking.

"Welcome, Bassi family. Welcome, Gisella. Nice to see you again. The whole team has been anxiously waiting for today, and we're so excited you could join us."

After hurriedly handing the tote to Gisella, Carolina stood between her dad and Chelsie. For once he wasn't wearing his old Padres baseball hat. She almost didn't recognize him without his mustache, and couldn't stop staring at him.

"What?" he mouthed at her, his cheeks reddening as if he were self-conscious.

She shrugged. "I like it," she whispered at him, clutching his hand.

Her heart felt like it was going to burst out of her chest, and maybe Papi sensed her nerves because he let go of her hand and wrapped an arm over her shoulder. Immediately, she felt more grounded.

The adults shook hands and exchanged kisses on the cheek. Carolina waited for her turn.

"Call me Estefanía," Mrs. Bassi said.

"I'm Edison," Gisella's dad added, shaking Carolina's hand.

Carolina was tongue-tied. She didn't think she'd seen Estefanía Bassi in the movies, but Gisella's mom was movie star gorgeous. She was tall and imposing, with sleek mahogany hair that fell to her hips. She had high cheekbones and soft amber eyes. But the best was her friendly smile.

"I heard she was Miss Venezuela once upon a time," Chelsie whispered in Carolina's ear.

Mr. Bassi had dark blond hair carefully combed to the

side, and smile wrinkles fanning from the corners of his eyes and mouth. He was a little shorter than Mrs. Bassi. Carolina had never seen a more striking family. They were dressed in simple clothes—jeans and sweaters, scarves and boots. Gisella already wore a purple Unbridled Dreams sweatshirt.

"We're matching," Carolina said to Gisella, trying to break the ice between them.

Gisella looked at her feet and then at her mom.

"Yes," Mrs. Bassi said. "We came in for a brief tour last week, and Gisella picked this one. Good choice, no?" she said in well-modulated English that still had the Caribbean flavor of Venezuela.

Carolina was still prickled that she had missed this visit last week, but she didn't have time to dwell on her own grievances.

"*You* picked it, Ma," Gisella cut in. Her voice was soft, but it had a chilling effect.

"But purple has always been your favorite color," Mr. Bassi said.

Gisella closed her eyes as if she were asking for patience. "It used to be, back in Miami. Now it makes me homesick."

There was an awkward silence. Mrs. Bassi's cheeks went bright red.

Carolina didn't completely understand what was going on, but she felt the tension in the air. She'd grown up at Paradise and lived in the same cottage since she was a baby. It was hard to understand what being homesick would be like.

But Chelsie did. She'd moved to the ranch a few months ago, and although she seemed happy and well-adjusted, Carolina knew she missed living in a big city.

"There are other colors you can choose, right, Caro?" Chelsie asked hurriedly.

Carolina nodded, wanting things to go back to the bubbly excitement of a few seconds ago.

Before Carolina darted to the storage room to grab a hoodie in another color, Mrs. Bassi and Gisella whispered in Spanish. Chelsie seemed to follow their conversation perfectly. But it moved so fast, and the words were so different from what Carolina spoke at home with her dad, that she hardly understood a thing. The grown-ups chimed in, using a mixture of English and Spanish that made Carolina feel out of the loop. She hadn't known Kimber was this fluent in Spanish too!

But then Chelsie said something that had Gisella's face lighting up. Chelsie nodded, her relief palpable. Even though Carolina didn't know what was going on, her shoulders dropped in relief too.

Kimber laughed at something Papi and Mr. Bassi said.

Carolina was bored of all this talking. She wanted to involve the stars of their show: the horses. Softly, she elbowed Chelsie, hoping her friend would get the signal.

Chelsie seemed to understand right away. "While they talk here, do you want to come see the little barn with us? You can meet the lesson horses and get some hands-on experience."

Gisella looked panicked, clutching her welcome gift bag, which she hadn't opened yet. She hadn't even peeked inside.

"I'm okay staying here, actually," she said, stepping closer to her dad. She sent her father a look that Carolina recognized as a call for help, to rescue her from this situation.

On the surface, everything seemed okay, but Gisella was . . . skittish.

And when a horse was skittish, the first thing to do was reassure it that everything was safe.

This time, Kimber swooped in before Carolina could try to take the reins. "Of course you can stay here. In that case, let me go over the course goals and expectations, and get these waivers signed."

Carolina followed along as Kimber read Gisella the Five Bs, and the contract about the student wearing a helmet and obeying directions at all times. Also, she explained how to go about rescheduling classes when needed, and went over the lesson plans that would extend from the second week of January until the end of March.

Then Gisella could have the choice to earn extra lessons if she volunteered doing chores at the barn.

Her jaw was set in a stubborn gesture that reminded Carolina of Twinkletoes when he refused to eat his special feed. But every time Gisella made eye contact with her parents or Kimber, she smiled, as if she were the happiest girl in the world.

What kind of sorrow did this girl hide behind her pretty smile?

Once they had gone over the paperwork, Mr. Bassi said to Gisella in Spanish, "I'll come get you in an hour's time." This time, he spoke slowly enough for Caro to understand.

Gisella turned toward him with urgency. This time there was no smile on her face. "Can you just wait for me here?" she asked in Spanish.

Kimber nodded and, looking at Gisella's parents, said, "Of course, you're welcome to wait for her."

But Mrs. Bassi shook her head. "I'm sorry, mi amor. We promised Mr. Sullivan we'd stop by the town hall to talk about the upcoming baseball season." She looked at Carolina, Chelsie, and Kimber. "Edison is in charge of organizing the youth leagues. He coached baseball in Venezuela, and it's a nice way to get to know our new community."

That made sense, Carolina thought.

"Okay, then," Kimber said with a clap. "Now, Carolina and Chelsie will introduce you to the lesson horses and show you how to take care of them. Then we can go on a little turn around the arena."

Gisella grabbed her mom's hand. "I don't want to ride a horse yet. I'm scared."

Carolina had not expected this.

The first student they were sponsoring was terrified of horses?

Had there been a misunderstanding somewhere?

Kimber didn't seem to appreciate the seriousness of this fact. If Gisella didn't even want to be here, what kind of feedback letter would she write to the donor? What if she wrote a bad review and then they had to close Unbridled Dreams?

"Don't worry," Chelsie said softly.

Carolina smiled at her friend and then she realized Chelsie had been trying to put Gisella at ease. That's what they needed to do, not panic like Carolina was doing.

"We'll go really slowly. You don't have to get on a saddle if you don't want to. But I promise you that soon enough, you're going to be counting down the hours to come to the barn," Chelsie said.

Gisella grimaced, like she doubted this would ever happen.

Carolina had to make an effort not to roll her eyes. Not at Gisella, necessarily, but at the situation.

The adults kept talking in Spanish, and Carolina didn't want to stand around to chitchat about the weather. She was itching to get busy!

"Let's go," she said, wishing her Spanish were better. She was so frustrated at herself! She should've introduced herself to Gisella at school. She should've kept up with her Spanish.

She led the girls out of the office, aware of the adults intently watching them, and Chelsie and Gisella whispering in Spanish a few steps behind her.

This was not the start she had been hoping for.

5

I'd Rather Be Dancing

Carolina pushed open the barn door with her shoulder and said, "Ta-da!"

"Welcome to the little barn!" Chelsie said, making a funny curtsy.

As if on cue, the horses—and one mini donkey—peeked out of their stalls to get a glimpse of the newcomer. Bella, the miniature painted horse, snorted like the diva she was.

Not to be outdone, Twinkletoes brayed so loud, the girls clasped their hands over their ears.

From the top of the rafters, Luna, the cat, growled.

It looked like these animals had never seen a human being before.

Carolina was shocked by their behavior.

"Want a hot chocolate, Gisella?" Chelsie asked as though to make up for the animals' welcome.

"You look so cold." Carolina rushed to close the barn door.

"We should've told you to bring your parka," Chelsie said. "These winters aren't for the faint of heart."

"Especially coming from Florida!" Carolina added and then winced. She hadn't meant to say Gisella was faint of heart, but was that how her words had sounded?

Flustered, she poured a cup of hot chocolate from the thermos they kept on a corner table and handed it to Gisella.

The new girl took a sip but got scalded. "Ouch!"

"Oh no!" Carolina exclaimed, watching helplessly as Gisella blew on her drink. "Sorry," she said sincerely.

Gisella tried to smile, but the gesture didn't seem convincing. Her lips looked bright red, while her face was fixed in a grimace. Her eyes darted about like she was assessing which direction to run.

"I've never been in a barn before," she said with pursed lips, brushing off still-green sprigs of hay that had gotten stuck to her black fleece pants already. "It smells . . . barn-y."

Chelsie laughed, but Carolina's first reaction was to get defensive. What had Gisella expected? Chanel No. 5? For being a place where animals lived, the little barn was clean and cozy. Chelsie's mom owned the whole property. But it had been Carolina's family who had worked at it for years and kept it afloat when the old owner stopped visiting and the riding school vanished into thin air. Heather owned most of the horses too, but the lesson horses down here were Carolina's dear old friends. That's how she thought of Paradise, as *hers*.

And she worked hard to keep her home at a top-notch level.

Chelsie got the broom to sweep away the hay, and Carolina bit her lip so as to not correct the way her friend held the handle. Her dad reminded her all the time that it didn't matter *how* things got done as long as the end result was right.

Chelsie had obviously never done barn chores before coming to Paradise, but one of the first things her mom did was insist that anyone who took lessons at the ranch had to learn all the chores. In order to ride, everyone had to know how to take care of the horses.

That's why this was the first part of the first lesson all Unbridled Dreams students had to do before they could even get on a horse. Chelsie's techniques were untraditional, but she got her chores done. Still, Carolina was worried she'd teach Gisella the wrong way to do things.

But Gisella didn't seem to be paying any attention to chores anyway. She looked at the CD cases on top of the table, and when she saw the cover of Velvet Lilly, she exclaimed, "This is my favorite album of all time! Can we play it?"

Chelsie beamed at her and put the music on. It wasn't the one Carolina had been listening to, so she didn't know any of the songs.

The girls talked about the concert Chelsie had attended, using a mixture of English and Spanish that Carolina couldn't follow. But when Carolina saw how Gisella was sweeping, she lost her patience. It was one thing not to have been around horses or other animals ever in her life, but had this girl never swept at home?

Carolina stomped to her side and said, "Actually, this is how you do it." She demonstrated sweeping toward her feet, just like Tyler had taught her a long time ago.

"And get my new shoes all dirty?" Gisella asked.

Carolina pointed to a footlocker near the entrance where there was an assortment of rubber boots in different sizes. "There," she said. "Change into a pair of those so you don't have to worry about ruining yours."

Gisella nodded but kept doing things her way.

"You need to clean toward you. Like this," Carolina said in what she hoped was a sweet teacher's voice. She demonstrated, but when she looked up, she saw Gisella rolling her eyes and Chelsie biting her lower lip.

"Or you can do it however you like to do it," she added in a small voice, handing the broom back to Gisella. The younger girl took the broom with one hand and pushed her hair back with the other. Carolina said, "Here's a hair elastic, in case you need it."

Gisella took it but put it in her pocket. "Thanks," she said. The tone in her voice indicated she was annoyed rather than grateful.

Carolina was desolate. She didn't know what she'd done wrong.

Chelsie came to the rescue, playing a different song and talking about the perfect choreo, whatever that was.

Feeling left out, Carolina couldn't help herself from straightening the rake and the squeegee on the hooks by the door. Then she turned to the stall by the feed room. Like always, she took refuge with the friends that never made her feel unwanted: horses.

Velvet nickered when she saw her approach, and Carolina's heart about melted. She handed her a treat inside a bucket and patted her impossibly soft nose. "I'll take you for a quick ride in the arena later, okay, girl?"

Velvet nodded as if she were saying yes.

"He's very pretty," Gisella said softly, but she still startled Carolina. She hadn't heard her approach Velvet's stall.

"It's she, actually. She's a mare, and yes, she's beautiful," Carolina said.

Gisella swallowed and licked her lips as if she didn't know what to say.

Carolina looked over her shoulder, but Chelsie was on her phone. She'd have to rescue this conversation herself.

But surprisingly, it was Gisella who broke the silence. "I didn't know I'd be the only student."

Carolina shrugged as she rummaged in her mind for the right thing to say. "You're not."

Gisella wrinkled her nose. "I meant today. I know Tessa is taking lessons. I thought she'd be here today."

At the name of Tessa, her other archnemesis and former best friend, Carolina felt like cold water was trickling down her back.

"Do you know Tessa?" she asked, trying to keep her opinion of Loretta's sidekick out of the conversation.

But still, there must have been something off in her voice because a tense atmosphere fell between the new girl and her—again.

Gisella's cheeks had a blush, but her eyes now were stormy and flashing. "Yes, she's my next-door neighbor. When I showed her the flyer for this program, she told me great things about Paradise Ranch. Why?"

Her voice was sharp and defensive. Carolina tried to appease her with her hands turned up as she said, "Nothing in particular, really. I was just asking." In fact, she had so many questions. "What made you apply for riding lessons? Is it something you always wanted to do?"

"I actually would've preferred dance lessons," Gisella said, her voice hitching with regret or longing, Carolina couldn't tell which.

"So why horses?" Chelsie asked, joining them again. She glanced at Carolina, who had been about to ask who in the world would prefer dancing to horses.

Gisella shrugged. "There is nothing else to do here."

Carolina almost choked on air.

"What? Nothing to do in Paradise?"

Ludicrous!

Their town and the whole state of Idaho was a world-class playground. That is, for people who loved the outdoors. Hiking, skiing, snowshoeing, canyoneering, paragliding, fly-fishing, hunting, camping. The list was endless. All things Carolina loved to do.

Nothing to do? She belly laughed so loud Twinkletoes started braying along with her.

Gisella twisted her finger around the tie of her hoodie as if she wanted to hide away like a turtle. A step behind her, Chelsie made a hand motion for Carolina to cut it.

"Hmm . . . What kind of dance do you do?" Chelsie asked, obviously trying to salvage the conversation.

Gisella turned toward Chelsie and said, "Flamenco," striking an elegant pose, her hands curling like doves above her high-held head.

The new girl wasn't shy at all. A shy person couldn't be so comfortable in their body, could they?

"Yes, too bad there's not flamingo around here," Carolina said, thinking about the one dance studio in town that taught everything from hip-hop to ballet. She was pretty sure they also did Irish dance. Her friend Vida had done that for a while. The wigs and dresses had been too much for Carolina, but she enjoyed the lively music.

"Flamenco," Gisella corrected. "Not flamingo."

"You're thinking of the bird, Caro," Chelsie said, her voice sounding like she was the one trying not to laugh now. "In Spanish, the word for the bird and the dance are the same: flamenco."

Carolina's shoulders dropped. "I knew that," she said with a tight smile.

Now Chelsie was making her feel like she didn't even speak Spanish. Caro tried to add something, but words were her enemy today when they shouldn't be. Her mom may have stopped teaching language arts a long time ago, but that didn't mean she'd stopped making sure Carolina's vocabulary was spelling-bee-champion level. Too bad Mom's Spanish wasn't up to par.

Gisella sighed, like she was bored, which brought Carolina back to her senses. She had to find common ground with the new student.

Love for Velvet was what had brought her and Chelsie together. Maybe Velvet could be that bridge with Gisella too.

"Do you want to brush her?" Carolina asked.

The turn of subject was abrupt, but both Gisella and Chelsie seemed relieved she'd brought this up.

"Why not the little one?" Gisella asked instead, turning toward Bella.

It was always the same. Everyone got charmed with the miniature horse.

"You can't ride Bella though," Carolina said, shrugging.

"She won't be riding Velvet either, Caro."

Chelsie had a point. Velvet wasn't a lesson horse.

"Actually, I think it's a great idea to start with a mini," Chelsie added, leading Gisella into the stall Bella shared with Twinkletoes, the mini donkey. The space was too cramped with Bella, the donkey, and the two girls. Grudgingly, Carolina stayed on the other side of the door in the aisle. She leaned on the post that divided the minis' stall and Velvet's and watched the new student gingerly stretching her hand to touch Bella's face.

"She's so soft," Gisella said, petting Bella's nose.

Chelsie picked up a hard rubber curry brush from a nearby bucket. "Here, brush her like this," she said, showing Gisella how to rub her coat the way Bella liked it, in circular motions.

At first, Carolina was jealous that Chelsie got to show her, but then seeing the smile on Gisella's face, Carolina's insides softened. No one could resist the loving look in a horse's eye and the softness of their nose. Even Gisella.

Caro shouldn't have taken things personally. What had she been thinking?

She wished she could have a do-over of the whole thing. Now thanks to Bella, they might have a chance to rescue the first lesson.

If Gisella didn't fall head over heels in love with the program, it would mean the ruin of Unbridled Dreams before it even started!

Gisella's application had been so compelling . . . That was the spirit Carolina wanted to bring into the lessons. She was determined that Gisella would forget she ever wanted to go to flamenco.

Chelsie and Gisella spoke in Spanish softly, and Carolina wanted to be part of their conversation. At the same time, she didn't want to ruin this moment of connection the girl had with Bella. It wasn't Velvet, but it was a bridge nonetheless.

Still, Carolina was envious.

Gisella had an accent in English. She spoke slowly but clearly, her enunciation perfect. Carolina wished her own Spanish was nearly as good as Gisella's English.

She counted with her fingers. She was second generation in the United States on her father's side, and the truth was that with the rest of the family so far away, the family spoke mainly in English, with only a few words of Spanglish sprinkled here and there.

Carolina understood almost everything in Spanish when her dad and Abuela Ceci spoke on the phone every Sunday afternoon, but obviously that wasn't enough to keep up with other people's quick convos. That didn't seem to be the case with Chelsie, who looked more Americanized than Carolina. But she spoke to her dad, who lived in Argentina, every day, and he insisted they speak in Spanish.

Even on that Chelsie had an advantage on her.

Caro petted Velvet's nose while the other two girls went through each brush with Bella. The mare nudged at Carolina, probably sensing the tension growing inside her. And then Bella shivered. She had the tickles.

Carolina couldn't help it anymore. She wanted to show Gisella the proper way to brush a horse's coat. She jumped inside the stall, took the brush from Chelsie's hand, and said in halting Spanish, "Actually, you have to use firm strokes so they don't get ticklish, you see?"

"Ticklish? Horses?" Gisella snorted.

"They totally get ticklish. But if you do it firmly like this—" She brushed Bella in a swift move, from the top of her withers to where her legs started. "They know you're in charge and you know what you're doing."

"But I don't know what I'm doing," Gisella said.

"Bella won't know that," Carolina said, exasperated.

Chelsie made that cutting sign again, but Carolina felt strongly Gisella had to learn this bit of advice. After all, being a good leader was the first B. She handed the brush to Gisella and said, "Now it's your turn. Show her you know what you're doing."

"Actually, now that you got brushing down," Chelsie cut in, "why don't we show you how to clean her hooves?"

Gisella wrinkled her nose. "Really?" she asked. "Is it

necessary that I learn to brush their hair and clean their hooves? How is that horseback riding?"

Carolina was about to say that riding started at the barn, but it was Chelsie who spoke first. "Grooming them gives you the chance to bond, to really get to know them. You'll see. Give it a try."

Chelsie demonstrated cleaning one of Bella's hooves, and then looked at Gisella.

Gisella inhaled as if gathering courage. Finally, she nodded and took the hoof pick Chelsie offered.

Carolina smiled. This was a big step!

But when Gisella tried to lift Bella's back leg, the mini wouldn't budge. There wasn't enough room in the stall for all of them, but Caro didn't want to miss a thing. Bella tried to turn away and whipped Gisella with her mane.

The new girl yelped, making Bella squirm even worse. Gisella looked scared.

"Maybe I don't want to do this, after all," she said, handing the brush back to Carolina. "They're so scary."

"Bella is the smallest horse we have." Carolina laughed. "If you're scared of her, then . . ."

But the new girl wasn't smiling.

"She has a diva attitude, but she's harmless. Ah! Bella, stop chewing my hair," Carolina said, waving her hand in the air, trying to stop Bella from eating her ponytail.

Gisella didn't say anything, but she didn't need to. She was eyeing Velvet, who looked very tall and intimidating in her stall. Bella, the miniature horse, tossed her mane over her shoulder like she was warning Gisella not to cross her.

Everything felt like a disaster and Carolina didn't know how to fix any of it.

The air was tense as Chelsie put away the grooming supplies.

"Why don't we finish grooming Velvet?" Carolina suggested, her voice trembling a little.

But Chelsie took a deep breath and said, "We're going to head to the big barn . . ." She left the intonation of the statement hanging like an invitation.

Chelsie's *we* seemed to mean her and Gisella. Carolina was invited, but Chelsie's tone implied... maybe Caro shouldn't come. Chelsie's forehead was wrinkled with worry, but Carolina didn't want to tell her now that she felt like the bad witch in a movie. No one needed to tell her that the first student of Unbridled Dreams hadn't taken to her. Gisella didn't like horses. That much was obvious. And clearly, she didn't like Carolina either. The old feeling of not being needed or, worse, wanted crept in although she tried to shoo it away. Hadn't Heather said repeatedly that there was room for everyone at Paradise? That there would always be a special place for Carolina? If so, why did she feel like all the work of the previous few weeks, preparing everything to be just perfect, had been for nothing?

Carolina felt a knot grow in her throat. She shook her head. "I'll finish here first. You go along for her ride in the arena."

Gisella was already outside.

"I don't know what happened," Chelsie said, wringing her hands. "Should we head to the big barn for the lesson? My mom made cupcakes. Red velvet, your favorite."

Carolina didn't feel like eating a cupcake. She felt like

running and running down the trail, far away to escape this feeling of doing everything wrong.

"You go ahead," she said, pushing her fists deep into her pockets. The list of her plans for today that she'd ripped out of the journal would be all wrinkled and ruined by now, but it didn't matter anymore. "See you later tonight right here at Velvet's stall?"

Ever since last year when they used to sneak in to say good night to Velvet while the barn slept, Carolina and Chelsie had the habit of stopping by the little barn as the day closed.

It was their favorite time to reconnect, and not only with the horse. Usually they didn't see much of each other at school. They were in different classes, and the rest of the time there was a lot of work to do.

At night, it was just the two of them cocooned in the warmth of sleepy horses, with only Luna as a witness, surveying them from her perch in the rafters.

"Are you sure?" Chelsie asked, so many conflicted emotions flashing in her eyes. "You're going to miss seeing her get in the saddle for the first time."

Carolina swallowed the knot in her throat and shrugged. "It's okay," she said although nothing could be further from the truth. "She's got you and Kimber. She's in good hands."

Chelsie stared at her for a second, but then a gust of wind blew hay from the feeders, messing up the floor again.

"Go before the horses catch cold," Carolina said, shooing Chelsie out the door where Gisella was waiting.

"See you tonight."

Carolina heard the crunch of the gravel as the girls went across the path and the parking lot to the big barn. The girls were laughing. Carolina ran to the window, and her heart twisted with jealousy when she saw Gisella and Chelsie shoulder to shoulder, already inseparable like best friends.

6

Almost Like a Centaur

Later that night, Carolina went back to the barn to hear all about Gisella and her lesson. Chelsie wasn't there yet. As if Abuelita Ceci were right next to her, Carolina could almost hear her singsongy voice say, "Just because you're early, it doesn't mean time will go faster, mamita."

She was about to head to the main house to find her friend, but then the door slid open.

Chelsie came in, hazel eyes blazing, leading Pepino, who had a funny look on his face too. At the sight of them, Luna jumped down to the floor and swept at Chelsie's legs with her paws.

"That means she missed you," Carolina said, laughing in spite of the sadness she still felt.

Chelsie tried to pet Luna, but the gray tabby cat ran up to the top of the bales of hay.

"She's so weird!" Chelsie said, shaking her head.

"She's a cat. She only wants to be loved on her own terms."

Chelsie crossed her arms and tapped her foot, looking at Carolina with a smirk on her face. "Reminds me of someone I know. Meow?"

Carolina blushed. "Stop it!"

She grabbed Pepino's lead rope from Chelsie and led him to his stall, which was right next to Velvet's, their meeting spot for their nightly ritual.

No matter what the day brought, Carolina loved this moment with the mare and her friend in the evening. Going over the day and making plans for the next one gave her a sense of new beginnings and possibility. Even if the winter days were short and dark, there were plenty of wonderful things to look forward to that lit up every moment. Maybe today would be the same.

She sat on a bale of hay and Chelsie joined her, draping an arm over her shoulder. Carolina let herself lean into her friend. Her heart drummed in anticipation. She was sure Chelsie would fill her in on the rest of Gisella's first day, and she wasn't disappointed.

"At first she didn't even want to get in the saddle," Chelsie said, and Carolina could see the whole thing unfold in her mind's eye. "She was on the verge of tears."

Carolina's insides twisted. She wished she had a time machine. She should've been there helping Gisella, not sulking in the little barn! Things would've turned out differently if she had gone with the girls.

But she was stubborn, and her ego had been wounded. She could be so intense sometimes. Last year when Orchard Farms became Paradise, she'd promised her dad that she'd think things through before reacting. She'd been so much better at it lately . . . until today.

At least Chelsie was here now, filling her in on all she had missed. "But Kimber is amazing, you know? She told her to just sit on Pepino without a saddle."

Carolina looked up. "What? That is . . . gutsy!"

She imagined what Gisella must have felt. Riding on a saddle was amazing because it gave you stability and a cushion. But also, when she'd ridden bareback—especially when she was little—it had made her feel like she was a centaur, part girl, part horse.

The power! The connection! The sense of freedom!

"And did she?"

Chelsie took gum from her pocket and offered a piece to Carolina. It was the best flavor, bubble gum, so she took one.

"She did, actually."

Carolina laughed, clapping her hands. "And what did Pepino do? Did he just stand there like a statue?"

Chelsie popped her gum and said, "He totally did. Which helped Gisella be more confident. At least she stopped shaking and actually smiled a little. Then Kimber and I took turns leading Pepino around the arena. By the end, she didn't want to get down."

Carolina glanced at Pepino and sighed. He shook his whole body like a dog, as if he were shaking off the day's work, and it kind of looked like he was smiling. What a good pony he was. He was in all his right to feel satisfied with himself.

"So . . . you think she'll be back next week for her lesson?" Even the animals seemed to hold their breath to hear Chelsie's reply.

"Definitely!"

Carolina felt relieved, but then she blushed again, feeling that Chelsie was staring at her. "What?"

"Next time she'll need an expert for groundwork," Chelsie said. "Once she connects before the ride, she'll be itching to get in the saddle. You know how it is."

She knew only too well. But, she admitted, "I'm not sure Gisella will want me there."

Chelsie narrowed her eyes and said, "Actually, she kept asking when you'd be coming back. It seems to me someone has a reputation for knowing the most about horses this side of the Mississippi, and she was disappointed she didn't get to see Carolina Aguasvivas in action."

Usually, when someone said Carolina had a "reputation,"

nothing positive followed. She was known as impulsive, hot tempered, loud.

Her kindergarten teacher had once said that even though she was tiny, the whole class felt the force of her personality as she walked in. She tried to make her personality smaller, but apparently, she never succeeded.

"She said that? Even though I snapped at her for sweeping the wrong way?"

"And you took the brush from her hand?" Chelsie said and then laughed.

Carolina tried to laugh too, but her eyes prickled with embarrassment. She covered her face with her hands.

Chelsie one-arm-hugged her and said, "She didn't say that with words, but she kept looking at the entrance, especially when she was able to complete a whole circle around the arena on her own. I mean, it took forever." She placed her hand over her mouth to muffle her voice and whispered, "She was on Pepino after all. But she did it. And she was proud."

"Well, she should be," Carolina said loudly. "Getting on a twelve-hundred-pound animal you're afraid of is a huge accomplishment! Well done, Pepino!" She jumped to her feet, full of energy again, and petted Pepino's mane. "You should be proud for being a patient, noble beast, my love."

Pepino nickered, and she gave him a treat. He deserved it.

And while they were at it, Chelsie helped her fill up the feed buckets for everyone. Twinkletoes twitched his tail like a happy dog.

"They sure eat so much more in winter," Carolina said.

"Would you rather eat something you hate every day but always feel full, or get to eat food that you love but always feel hungry?" Chelsie asked, sounding like Bracken.

"I'm a growing girl," Carolina said, flexing her biceps. Her voice didn't sound like Bracken's, but she nailed the facial expression.

They both burst into laughter.

"I hate to admit it, but even when he's not here, he's still here. You know what I mean?" Carolina said, brushing her hands on her jeans.

"How did Paradise ever exist without him?" Chelsie said, filling up the water troughs for the night.

Twinkletoes snorted with gratitude as he chased a mouthful of hay with a drink.

Like every night, Carolina and Chelsie stretched this moment in the little barn as late as they could. But like all things, good and not so good, it came to an end. Chelsie's phone buzzed in her pocket.

"Oh well, I have to go back. See you tomorrow."

"See you tomorrow. Night, Chels. Don't worry. I'll get the lights."

Chelsie left.

Alone again, but in better spirits, Carolina took the paper out of her pocket. She smoothed out the crease lines. She'd written so many things she wanted to share with the first student. She'd imagined this day so differently!

But Gisella's journey through Unbridled Dreams had only just begun. And tomorrow would be a better day. Hopefully Carolina's ride tomorrow with Shadow would be better too.

Shadow . . .

What was she going to do with him?

Then a lightbulb seemed to turn on. If riding bareback

worked to connect Gisella with Pepino, it could certainly work to help Carolina bond with Shadow too, right?

She couldn't wait to try it. Perhaps that way, she would figure out why he was so unbalanced.

With a smile on her face, Carolina headed back to her house at the top of the hill.

7

It's Not Personal

For all Carolina's good intentions, she wasn't able to try her bareback experiment with Shadow right away. Kimber hadn't wanted her to do it without close supervision, and the trainer had been busy all week. Things between girl and horse didn't get much better. In fact, their relationship went from bad to worse.

Every time they did groundwork exercises, he refused to join up with her. Every time anyone else tried, he complied happily, all the while sending Caro what she thought was a smug smirk.

Finally, the following Wednesday evening, she was able to try riding bareback. Perhaps Carolina and this stubborn horse wouldn't become soul mates, but at least she didn't want to end up feeling like she should quit trying to become a horse-woman and switch to . . . dance or something.

"Are you ready?" Kimber asked as she took the saddle and pads off Shadow. "You know I won't let you go faster than a walk, and I'll be holding on to the halter all along."

As if to add his own warning to the trainer's words, Shadow flicked his mane against Caro's face. Chelsie, who was sit-ting over on the stands, tried not to chuckle when Carolina snorted with frustration. Even Kimber seemed like she was trying not to laugh.

Perhaps this wasn't such a good idea after all.

"You can do it, Caro!" said Chelsie, Carolina's very own cheerleader.

Carolina sighed, and squaring her shoulders, she headed to the mounting block. She didn't mind sticking to a walk, but did Kimber really have to hold the halter like Carolina was two years old? She hadn't dared protest, but maybe Shadow was picking up on her attitude because as soon as she hopped on his back, he stiffened.

Her seat wasn't as comfortable as on a saddle, of course, not with his bony withers and spine under her. But she placed her hands on his neck and whispered, "Be my friend, Shadow."

The gray Arabian's skin was warm, and she felt like a current of electricity buzzed between them as he breathed in and out with each stride he took. She turned her head toward Chelsie, and following the shift of her weight, he turned in that direction too.

Instinctively, she tightened the grip of her legs, and he seemed ready to spring. But Kimber was prepared. "Easy, Shadow," the trainer said, and then looked over her shoulder at Carolina and instructed, "Let your legs hang loose. No pressure or he'll think you're telling him to move into a higher gear."

Carolina tried to. She really did. But habits aren't easy to switch on and off. She felt like Shadow was gliding over the ground, and not used to the sensation of feeling each of the muscles of his back shift, she wanted to hold on to something.

"Grab his mane. You know it won't hurt him," Kimber said.

Carolina did know this, and she grabbed a thick strand of his mane.

"Don't use it like a video game joystick though," Kimber added without even looking at what Carolina was doing.

"How do you know?" she asked, perplexed.

The trainer shook her head. "I just know."

Maybe one day, Carolina would achieve that level of expertise as a horsewoman. But that day wasn't today. She kept tightening her legs around Shadow's girth. The only result was a jarring stop-and-go that had Carolina sweating in frustration. Soon, Shadow was sweating too, even though they'd only walked one circle around the arena.

When Shadow started steering to the mounting block, now also ignoring the trainer's directions, Kimber said, "Maybe you can try again tomorrow." Perhaps she too was starting to get tired—and even frustrated—with this tug-of-war.

Carolina agreed. She slid off Shadow's back and started to stomp away.

"Thank you, Shadow," Kimber said in a tone that stopped Carolina in her tracks.

She turned around and repeated in a monotone, "Thank you, Shadow."

Kimber nodded, but Shadow ignored her. Carolina trudged across the sandy footing.

Chelsie met her at the gate of the arena. "Don't let him get to you, Caro. It's not personal."

"It's kind of hard not to," Carolina replied. She tried not to let jealousy leak into her words.

Chelsie's class with Velvet had been right before Caro's. They'd been trotting and cantering and even jumping poles. Well, maybe just one pole that rose barely inches from the ground, but still.

And here she was, struggling to get a basic join-up and a walk around the arena.

He was so stubborn!

Though Carolina wanted nothing more than to storm away to the cottage, she had to wait for Kimber's final instructions. But when the trainer walked up to Carolina, she only asked her to put Shadow away for the night.

"Can I take care of Velvet instead?" she asked.

"Who's going to take care of Shadow?" Kimber asked.

Carolina was tempted to suggest maybe the trainer could do it, but seeing the expression on her face, she didn't dare to. "Chelsie?" she asked instead.

Kimber sent her a look that made Carolina gulp. "Sorry," she said.

"Sooner or later, you and Shadow have to make your peace with each other."

The words resonated in Caro's mind as she went through the motions of grooming Shadow in the big barn where he spent his nights. She relived every moment of the lesson, unable to figure out what she could've done differently. A horse in a nearby stall snorted, taking her out of the whirlwind of her thoughts and bringing her back to the present.

Shadow stared at her as she stood next to him with the curry brush in her hand. She'd been brushing his back thoughtlessly for a few minutes. The familiar ritual after a ride hadn't left her the closure she expected.

She was about to open her heart up to Shadow, ask him what was wrong between them. But in that moment, he tossed his mane and flicked her face with the coarse hair.

"Suit yourself," she said.

Without even a good-night kiss on his nose or a pat on his back, she stepped out of the Arabian's stall and latched it behind her.

Impulsively, Carolina headed to the little barn, tacked up Pepino, and took him into the arena for a short ride. She needed a dose of fun. But her mind wasn't in the saddle. She already regretted walking out on Shadow without even looking at his face, but it was too late. Pepino was a sweetheart though. He didn't go very fast, but at least he obeyed her.

Now that her temper had cooled down, Carolina was determined to ask her dad for his opinion. He was mostly self-taught, but he had the fabled family magical touch with horses. He might have a pointer she could use to fix her relationship with the stubborn gelding.

8

What the Blizzard Brought

The cottage was dark and cold. At the end of the day, when Carolina arrived home after chores, warm orange flames usually danced in the fireplace. Now, without the comforting coziness of a fire and the sounds of her parents going about their business of running the ranch, the house felt like a strange place. Carolina was disappointed her parents were gone, but not really surprised. They were so busy this time of the year, and even though now there were more people helping at the ranch, coming home to an empty house was still a possibility.

She took a hot shower, hoping the water and her favorite strawberry foamy soap would wash away more than grime from the stables. After she'd changed into flannel pajamas, she was in a better mood. Until she went down to the kitchen.

When she put Pepino away, it had started to snow. But now, big fat flakes flashed by the window like mini shooting stars. The roads would be slick and dark, a dangerous combination.

Her parents still hadn't arrived.

Caro's mind started spinning into what-if scenarios. As she dialed her mom's number, she tried to shoo the thoughts away before they could get ahold of her and make her more anxious. The call went straight to voicemail.

Maybe because she was an only child, she was very close to her parents. And now with Unbridled Dreams, she and her mom had become much, much closer.

Jen Aguasvivas had been a teacher before she had married Amado and moved from California to Idaho with him and baby Carolina. She kept the barn's financial books and made sure all the numbers were in order. She had worked so hard to make sure the donations stretched like a rubber band to cover everything for the first student at Unbridled Dreams! Jen didn't love horses the way Carolina and her dad did, but she knew the benefits of working with them. The special journal had been her idea. She'd been fired up with the enthusiasm of working on printing everything out and preparing the gift bags and other details like a feedback box so that everyone at Paradise Ranch could make suggestions to make things better.

So far, the only people to leave feedback had been Loretta, Bracken, and Chelsie.

Loretta had complained about everything, including that the helmets were too small for her head. Kimber showed her how to arrange her hair so the helmet fit better.

Bracken's note had been anonymous, but the question gave him away. "Would you rather lower the age limit to include under-tens or not?"

Carolina had written a big *No* and pinned the paper to the bulletin board. When Bracken saw it, his shoulders slumped.

"Don't wish the years away," Chelsie had told him in a know-it-all voice. "You'll be ten before you can believe it."

"But why ten?" Bracken asked. "Who made that irrational and painful decision to leave me out?"

Carolina wiggled her eyebrows and replied, "Because it

gives you something to look forward to and because Kimber said so."

Kimber had been adamant on placing an age limit for the Unbridled Dreams students. No under-tens—yet. Double digits had never seemed like a big deal to Carolina, but for Bracken, they were everything.

Chelsie's note had been "Can we also have soda in the snacks fridge?"

Heather had traced *No soda* in big red letters and pinned it to the bulletin board. "Not only are you nourishing your psyche and spirit when you ride, but also your body. And let's be honest: Soda isn't the best thing to drink after working hard on a ride."

At her words, JC, one of the stable hands, hid his glass bottle of soda behind his back. His mom sent him the bottles in a special delivery every month from Mexico. He couldn't find his favorite kind in Idaho.

In spite of her fear for her parents' safety, this memory made Carolina smile. She was sure they were okay. It wasn't really that late, just dark. They were only taking a long time to arrive because Papi was always extra careful in the snow. Carolina's stomach grumbled, but she wanted to eat dinner with her family. She grabbed a packet of beef jerky from the pantry and sat down to watch YouTube videos of Tina Hodges and Milo Sánchez, Chelsie's dad. They were the next best thing besides getting advice from her dad.

What to do about Shadow?

She sighed . . .

Carolina had never been in this situation before. She didn't know how to sort out her feelings of frustration. She hadn't believed it would ever be possible that she'd meet a horse that didn't become her best friend right away. After all, didn't she have the legendary Aguasvivas magic touch?

Where was it when she needed it the most?

But nothing Tina or Milo said helped her feel like she could get out of the war of wills with Shadow. One video led to another, and soon she went down the rabbit hole of horse videos in which the theories started contradicting each other.

Go with the flow clashed with *Make sure the horse understands who the boss is.*

That last one resonated more with her. After all, being the boss was the first guiding principle of Unbridled Dreams. It meant that if you were in control of your emotions, you'd be more capable of making the right decisions. At least you'd be making them from a place of conviction. And if the horse sensed their rider was confident, they would trust the rider. Was that it? Was the problem that Shadow didn't trust her?

And then she remembered Gisella's second lesson was coming up, and her heart sputtered with nerves. They hadn't really crossed paths at school at all these last few days, and Carolina was anxious about the next time they would see each other.

Carolina closed the computer with a snap.

Why couldn't life be simpler? Why didn't new friendships and horses operate under the same rules?

The sound of her dad's truck coming up the road shook her out of her downward spiral.

She jumped to her feet right as her mom was coming through the front door, a blazing smile on her face.

"Mami!" Carolina exclaimed, running to hug her.

No matter how different they were from each other, Carolina's mom was her safe haven.

Her mom hugged her tightly and kissed Carolina's forehead. Her lips were cold.

"Is the storm any worse?" Carolina asked.

Her mom shivered but took her coat off and hung it up on the coat rack next to the fireplace, and started to light a fire.

"It's a blizzard," her mom said. Her phone chimed, and when she looked at it, she added, "Sorry I didn't get your call. Signal was terrible!"

"I was trying not to get worried," Carolina said, but even now she felt concerned about the sounds coming from outside. Her dad was talking but she couldn't tell what he was saying. "Where were you guys? Who is out there with Papi?"

She walked to the window, but she couldn't see anything.

"Come here," her mom said.

She had a twinkle in her eye that made Carolina think of Christmas or birthdays, when something big was about to happen and Mom couldn't wait for Carolina to find out.

Thoughts of Gisella and cantering and Shadow went out the window. At least for now.

"What is it?" she asked, jumping in place with excitement.

She walked toward the door, but her mom held her back. "Be patient. You'll know soon enough."

Carolina's heart was going to beat right out of her chest.

When she couldn't contain her expectation any longer, she looked at her mom pleadingly and said, "What is it, Mom? Who is it? I can't stand waiting."

Her mind couldn't even imagine what the surprise would be. But judging by her mom's rapturous expression, she knew it had to be something—or someone—very special.

Could it be Abuela Ceci coming to visit them finally? Abuela was scared of flying, but it had been so long since they'd been together, maybe she'd decided to surprise them. She had promised that one way or another, she'd come to Paradise. Had she driven the whole way from New Mexico where she lived with Uncle Achilles and Aunt Julie?

But before she could ask her mom if that was the surprise, the door opened.

A gust of polar wind swept through the kitchen. The fireplace flames danced, revived by the air. The papers ruffled on the table and the kitchen bulletin board. Carolina's wild curly hair flew in her face. She hurried to wipe it out of her eyes when she heard her dad's footsteps walking into the house.

Her dad wore the giant parka he reserved for doing chores outside in the winter. She could hardly see his face, surrounded by the faux fur of the hood, until he unzipped and peeled open his jacket.

Inside was a dog. A sleeping puppy.

Carolina stared at its perfect face. The black-and-white dog was no bigger than Luna the cat. But it was fluffier than even a stuffed animal. It was the most adorable creature she'd ever seen, and out in the country, she saw adorable creatures on the daily.

She couldn't help it. She shrieked.

"Shhh," her dad said.

Carolina clapped her hands over her mouth, and she realized she was shaking. And not because of the cold that was still swirling around the kitchen.

She'd wanted a dog all her life.

"Is she ours?" she asked. "Are we keeping her?"

"It's a he. And yes, we're keeping him. At least that's the plan."

Her dad placed the dog on the floor. The puppy flinched when his paws touched the cold tile, and he blinked as he awoke from his nap. With halting footsteps, he walked right up to Carolina, who was kneeling with her arms wide open, and he licked her face, sealing the instalove that had bloomed in her heart.

He loved her too.

A dog!

Her first dog ever.

9

Boo!

Carolina couldn't stop kissing the puppy. His ice-blue eyes were hypnotic, and when he yawned, his pink tongue peeked through tiny teeth and sharp canines. The dog whined.

"Is he okay?" Carolina asked, noticing that he seemed uncomfortable.

In reply, the dog squatted and peed on the floor.

Carolina screamed, amused and horrified at the same time.

"I guess he's marking up his territory," Mom said with a twist of her mouth.

Papi threw his head back and laughed and laughed. The emotions of the last few days had been so all over the place that before she could stop herself, she burst into tears.

A dog! A dog for *her*.

"Aw," Papi said, pulling her close into the refuge of his arms. "Come here, Llorona."

"I'm not crying!" Carolina said, half sobbing, half laughing, soaking his flannel with fat, hot, happy tears.

All her life, she'd begged her parents to let her get a puppy. When Loretta and Carolina were in kindergarten, Loretta had gotten a dog and Carolina had wanted its sibling. Mom had said she was still too young to take care of an animal, but soon, when Carolina started working at the barn like one of the ranch hands, it became pretty obvious that she had all the skills needed to take care of herself and other living beings.

But then there had been a serious incident at the ranch. Carolina had seen the whole thing. One of Mr. Parry's horses had gotten spooked by a visitor's dog. It had been a Labrador, so no one had thought anything of it when, instead of waiting in the car, it jumped through the narrow opening in the window.

To this day, she couldn't believe a dog had been able to

squish its body like a mouse and escape through the cracked window. Or how fast it ran toward the horses when it saw them in the big pasture.

Or how terrified the horses were.

Sometimes at night she woke up with the fearful scream of that poor horse, running like the wind, trying to get away from that dog and its sharp fangs. Horse, dog, and owner had been hurt. The horse's flank had an ugly gash that took weeks to heal. The dog had a bruised skull from when the horse had kicked it trying to defend himself. And the owner ended up with a broken friendship with Mr. Parry, who had immediately banned all dogs from the property.

Never again had a dog been seen in the pasture or the arena.

With time, Carolina had stopped thinking she could get her own dog. Horses were enough to keep her company. But then again, she couldn't have a sleepover in her room with one. Not even Twinkletoes or Bella, the minis. To start with, Bella's ego alone wouldn't fit in the cottage on top of the hill, and for seconds, they would poop all over the place!

Her parents started to look at her with concern when her

sobbing turned intense, so she tried to stop crying. But that's the thing with emotions. Sometimes when they're locked in for a while, they explode like waterfalls and fireworks—or a volcano.

"A dog?" Carolina said, and she hiccuped. "Why? How?"

She glanced at the calendar. It wasn't a second Christmas now, was it? Or maybe it was a holiday she didn't know about? Three Kings' Day had been a couple of weeks ago, and she'd received a new pair of riding gloves from her parents and a turquoise ring in the mail from Abuela Ceci.

Mom and Papi hugged her. The first hug of their family of four, and Carolina basked in the moment.

She would let them believe her tears were all due to happiness. She wouldn't tell them that mixed in were tears from being so sad and disappointed that Gisella didn't seem to like her. That for the first time in her life, she hadn't clicked with a horse. Shadow was making her doubt all her skills, and she didn't know how to deal with that.

Her dad headed to the kitchen to get paper towels and

disinfectant to clean up the puppy's puddle, and Mom kept one arm around Carolina, who in turned looked at the puppy as if it were a miracle.

Now that her eyes were a little drier, she realized that, yes, it was a puppy, but not newborn.

"He's six months," Papi said, wielding paper towels in front of him, probably guessing the questions she had.

"Six months? Is he fully grown? He's small, isn't he?"

The questions rolled off her tongue like snowflakes falling from heavy clouds.

"He seems like he's a small breed," Mom said. "Maybe a mix of Australian shepherd and corgi."

"Maybe a miniature husky," her dad said, studying the puppy's face. Papi didn't seem to be able to stop smiling either. He was such an animal lover!

"He's a mix like me!" Carolina exclaimed, extending her arms wide.

Her parents laughed.

"You're right," Mom said. "The lady at the shelter said he

might be fully grown, but who knows what surprises he has for us."

"I think he's perfect," Carolina said, plopping onto the floor and reaching out her hand for the puppy.

He sniffed the air, and maybe he could smell the beef jerky on her hand, or maybe he just really liked her and wanted to say hi. Either way, he walked tentatively forward and licked her fingers.

Tickles ran like a current through her whole body. With the current, her heart melted. She was absolutely in love with a creature she hadn't even known existed a few minutes ago. How strange love is. How strange and magical. She didn't know how it had happened. How to replicate it. But for now, she accepted it with a humbled heart.

"Come here, sweetheart," she said.

The puppy walked up to her and snuggled on her lap, where he curled up and yawned as if he needed to go to sleep right that instant. His hot breath didn't smell sweet like milk, as a young puppy's might, but she didn't care. Not even when she realized he'd shed a few white hairs on her dark fleece pajama pants. What did it matter that he shed? She was always covered in horsehair anyway.

Loretta didn't tease her about it anymore now that she too had horsehair sticking out of her own head. But for a while, she'd been ruthless with Carolina, who would spend inordinate amounts of time making sure there was no hair or speck of dirt on her clothes so the mean girls at school wouldn't torment her. Usually, it proved impossible.

"Tell me all about him, please! Why you decided to bring a dog home now," she said, sniffling the leftover tears. She wanted to know the whole story. "And what is Heather going to say?"

Mom, who'd put a casserole in the oven, placed some chips and salsa on the table. She too sat down to hear the story.

Papi scratched his curly hair and smiled like a little boy. "A few weeks ago before Christmas, I had to stop by the shelter to talk to Dr. Rooney."

Dr. Rooney was the veterinarian. He'd encouraged Tyler to go to college, to help him with his practice someday in the future.

"How is he doing?" Mom asked.

Papi nodded. "You know he's happiest when he's among animals. He didn't say much, but I could tell his back still hurt."

"Did he fall from a horse?" Carolina asked. Dr. Rooney was a skilled horseman.

Papi shook his head. "He threw out his back playing golf, of all things."

"He's going to love getting Tyler back to help him," Carolina said, scratching the spot between the puppy's ears. He seemed to love that. He had an expression like he was smiling, and in turn it made her smile too.

"Dr. Rooney was attending to a little cat mama that had a litter of kittens out in the cold. Someone found them and brought them to the shelter. I almost took him up on the request to foster some kittens or even get one for the big barn. Luna is getting pretty chunky, with her monopoly on the mice population to snack on."

Carolina had seen Luna hunting for mice the first time she'd snuck out to visit Velvet at night. She shivered at the memory of the mouse's squeal coming from her jaws.

"Why didn't you bring home a kitten?" Mom asked. She'd been wanting a house cat to keep her company.

Papi sighed. "Actually, one of the usual foster parents came back early from Christmas vacation and was ready to take all seven of them in, including the mom. I know we could've learned to take care of little kittens. How hard can it be?" he asked. "But I think that situation was better for them. They were all as tiny as mice themselves. Besides, there was this dog that started barking, and something in my heart started whispering that perhaps it had been waiting for me."

Carolina looked at her dad. "How so?"

Papi shrugged with a fond smile. "He started calling for me the moment I walked in. Dr. Rooney and I could hardly talk. Katherine, the main desk receptionist—you know, Dr. Rooney's wife?—was surprised."

"Why?" Caro asked.

"They'd received the dog three weeks ago, and Dr. Rooney hadn't had the heart to transfer him to the animal shelter yet," her dad said.

The closest animal shelter was several miles from Paradise,

so this was a common occurrence. Katherine had once said they'd be living in a menagerie if it was up to her husband. He wanted to keep all the animals that crossed his path.

"Why did the family surrender him?" Caro asked.

"They were moving to an apartment in Boise, or something like that, and couldn't take him."

"Or didn't want to take him," Mom added with a shake of her head.

Carolina shivered, thinking about what it must be like to love someone for months of your young life and then be apart from them.

"Poor puppy! He must have missed his family so much!"

Papi scratched his hair again. "That's the thing: They had thought he couldn't speak—I mean, bark. He never made a sound. Not even a whine at night. But as soon as he heard me, he wouldn't stop barking. So I did what any other person would do when a good boy calls."

"What?" Carolina asked, imagining the whole thing like it was a movie playing in her mind. She could even imagine the emotional piano music in the background.

"I peeked inside and once he saw me, his tail wagged so hard he hurt himself when he wacked it against the floor with all his might." Papi laughed, lifting the puppy in his arms like he was Simba being introduced to the whole animal world on the savanna.

"Katherine told me the doctor thought he was going to let himself die of sadness. He had never been interested in anyone, even with so many people looking for a Christmas pet."

"Poor thing!" Mom said.

"And that day I left but I've been thinking about him ever since."

"Why didn't you bring him home for Christmas?" Carolina asked, a little outraged that she'd missed weeks with this beauty.

This year Christmas had been so fun with Chelsie and Heather and Kimber. They had been preparing the last details of Unbridled Dreams, so they'd seen each other every day. But a dog among them would've been magical.

"I wanted to clear it by Heather first," he said.

"I'm sure she won't have a problem!" Carolina exclaimed, and then her face fell. "Or do you think she'll have us send him back?"

Papi shook his head. "She said that the dog was welcome. Especially a working dog."

"A working dog?" She eyed him suspiciously. The dog had fallen asleep belly up, a drunken expression on his face that made Carolina laugh.

"Of course, he's too little now," Papi said. "But it seems like he comes from working-dog stock. And working dogs are the happiest when they have a job."

"And what will his job be? Protecting the horses?"

Papi shook his head. "I know he'll protect them and us if needed. But mainly, his job is to be a companion. In the spring, we'll be starting horseback country and canyon rides with tourists again. Remember we talked about it last year?"

"Yes!" Carolina exclaimed, and she jumped in the air, waking up the puppy. He sent her an accusing look and then went back to sleep.

In her defense, she loved being a guide on trail rides. She'd been on a few with her dad, who let her come along, especially if there were children in a group.

"I'd love for the dog to learn to run and be a trailblazer. Check out the path for us, scare away squirrels and snakes or any other critters that might spook the horses and create a hazard for the tourists riding with us."

Carolina saw herself under the blazing sun, guiding a train of people and horses under the canopy of the trees and the occasional bald eagle flying above. She would lead confidently on a horse who she loved and who loved her back. If she added a dog by her side, what else could she ask for? Life would be perfect.

"And does he already know how to do that? Has he been exposed to horses and a farm before?" she asked.

"That was my question too," Mom said.

"We don't know anything about him yet," Papi said. "We don't know how he lived before the shelter. What kind of training he had, if any."

"He did pee on the floor," Carolina said because he'd done that with the confidence of a champ. "We know he's not housebroken."

"Yes, but in his defense," Mom said, "we had a long drive, and he didn't go before we left for the road. It might also be his excitement about meeting you."

Carolina sent the puppy an adoring look.

"I guess we'll see how fast he learns," Papi said. "Little by little, we'll introduce him to the horses and the other animals. And then we'll teach him basic commands. Like sit, stay, and come."

"Easy!" said Carolina, slapping her thigh for emphasis. "I'll have him fully trained by spring or my name isn't Carolina Rose Aguasvivas."

"Are you sure?" Papi asked. "You have school and the clinic and house chores. Do you want to be his main trainer too?"

Did she ever?

Of course! She had been ready her whole life.

Papi and Mom looked at each other, having one of their silent conversations that got resolved by the time Carolina blinked.

"If you're up to it, then the job is yours," Papi said, clapping his hands as if there was nothing else to discuss.

Mom said, "Now, before we eat dinner, there's an important piece of information we haven't resolved: his name."

Carolina perked up. She'd never named a pet herself. Not even Luna. She'd already been around by the time Carolina learned to say her own name.

She observed the dog. He had an ear twisted and his tongue lolling out of his long, skinny mouth. He was black with a white face, and had white patches all over his body, but the one around his crystal-blue eyes was black.

"Spot?" Mom suggested.

"Panda?" Papi said.

He reminded Carolina of a pirate, or someone playing peekaboo.

Boo!

It had a fun ring to it!

"What about Boo?" Carolina replied.

"I love it!" her mom said.

Papi laughed and said, "What do you think, Boo? Is that your name?"

The dog opened his eyes and whined, as if saying he loved it.

"Doo it is, then! Welcome to Paradise!" Carolina exclaimed.

She gathered the puppy in her arms.

That night, they slept in each other's arms and paws.

10

Puppy 101

Carolina woke up to a little pink tongue washing her face with kisses. She couldn't have imagined a sweeter way to return to reality.

The feeling of a warm, fluffy puppy next to her while a snowstorm raged outside was so comforting, she didn't understand how no one had prescribed it for her chronic winteritis before. Why had she not insisted on getting a dog much, much sooner than this?

Her alarm wouldn't be blaring for a while, but after the puppy kisses, she was completely awake.

She gazed toward the window. The snow fell hard and heavy. The ride to school would be *interesting*. If it weren't for the fact that her friend Vida would be waiting for her on the bus, and the promise of the surprise on Vida's face when she found out Caro finally had a dog, she'd be tempted to stay home today.

"Ah, time to get up," she said to Boo. He panted at her happily and yawned with a tiny squeal. Carolina also had chores ahead of her. She couldn't wait to introduce Boo to the rest of her animal friends. And Chelsie of course.

She swung her legs out of bed and stepped in . . . a puddle.

"Eww! What in the world?"

If dogs blushed, Carolina was sure Boo would be pinking up so hard right now his face would glow in the dark. He whined and covered his eyes with a paw. It was so adorable, Carolina couldn't help but ruffle his fur and kiss his black nose.

"We need to work on potty training ASAP," she said, trying to find the silver lining in this situation. She ran to the bathroom—hopping on one foot with a grimace—and grabbed a wipe to clean the floor. Good thing her floors were hardwood or else she'd be doomed. She'd read somewhere that it's pretty much impossible to get the scent off carpets or rugs.

She got dressed for chores and was ready to go out when she remembered the puppy. Boo was sound asleep again on her bed.

Little stinker. He'd kept her up half the night until she had finally let him climb into bed with her. She'd told him he could sleep at the foot of the bed, but somehow, he'd ended up with his head on the pillow. There were hairs all over that couldn't be Carolina's—unless she'd gotten super old overnight and sprouted grays already. She suspected the puppy.

"Let's go, Boo," she said.

This time Boo didn't whine or try to earn her sympathy. He blinked skeptically, like he couldn't believe she had the nerve to try to get him out of bed in this weather.

"Come on, sleepyhead," she said, petting him. "You're the one who woke me up. Lots of work ahead of us today."

Boo ignored her. Or maybe he'd already fallen back to sleep and entered doggy dreamland.

She picked him up and carried him downstairs.

Mom sent them both a smile. "Good morning," she said,

putting her coffee mug down. "I heard someone whining last night. Did he finally sleep well?"

Carolina nodded, but before she could reply, she yawned so widely her jaw made a funny popping sound.

Mom laughed. Boo groaned like he was asking them to be quiet please, which made Carolina laugh too.

"I better take him outside."

"I'll get your toast ready," Mom said.

Carolina stepped out through the back door. The cold hit her like a slap. She carefully placed Boo on the snow-covered grass. She knew underneath the snow there was sleeping green. Sleeping spring and summer. Sleeping life. She couldn't wait for the warm weather to arrive, but she was grateful for the snow too.

The last few years, it hadn't snowed very much, and then in the summer months, there were terrible brush fires that threatened communities of people and animals alike.

Luscious green pastures and babbling brooks happened because of snow. There wasn't one without the other.

Boo stood there, half asleep himself, looking at her like he didn't understand what she wanted him to do.

"Go like this," she said, mimicking lifting her leg.

Still, he watched her.

"You already went inside . . ." she said, scratching her head.

She picked him back up and returned to the kitchen. As soon as Carolina placed him on the floor, he squatted and peed.

"What?" she exclaimed.

She hadn't intended to yell or sound harsh. But Boo got scared. He looked up at her through his long lashes, his head ducked between his pointy shoulders, a heartbreaking expression of shame on his face.

"Oh no," Mom said, handing Carolina another disinfectant wipe and a dry paper towel to clean the floor. "It seems he doesn't like sudden loud noises."

"I'm sorry, Boo," Carolina said, already regretting not having waited patiently outside even for one more minute.

Boo licked her hand as if he accepted her apology. She

cleaned the floor and washed her hands, and when she started eating breakfast, she realized Boo was sitting in front of her, looking at her so intently she could practically read his mind.

Food, his eyes said.

She hesitated for a second before she offered him a piece of toast.

"I wouldn't do that if I were you," Mom said with a knowing voice. "Once you give in the first time, it'll be pretty impossible to break bad habits."

But Boo was already licking the crumbly vestiges of the buttered bread.

"I guess we need to train him," Carolina said, but the whole time she knew she had no idea what that actually meant. She didn't know how to train a dog. No clue. What had she been thinking when she'd promised she'd have him ready by spring?

"I'm sure he also has some bad habits from his other home. Cowering from raised voices might be because they were very harsh with him."

"Poor Boo!" Carolina said, kneeling on the floor for her to better kiss him.

He playfully bit her hand. His teeth were extra sharp, like the little thorns of wild roses. She knew she had to stop using her hand as a chew toy with him, and she told herself next time she'd do better.

"I'm taking him for chores," she said.

"Are you sure?" Mom asked from the sink. "I'll watch him if you want."

But Carolina couldn't bear leaving him behind. She was actually already wondering if she could just stay home— forever. Homeschooling again, like she'd done in third grade, sounded like a great idea. But then she wouldn't see Vida and Gisella, and she would be out of the loop like she'd been once upon a time. The FOMO was real. From both options.

She put a hat on, grabbed the puppy, and headed outside again. In her mind she went over all the supplies she needed to train Boo. She needed a leash pronto. He snuggled against her shoulder, looking behind them with his paws around her neck.

"I have the best scarf in the whole wide world," she said. "Maybe if you remain this calm, you could come with me to school. I'm sure the teacher won't notice."

She laughed as she opened the door to the little barn. Velvet Lilly was already sounding from the boom box.

"Good morning, my loves," she greeted everyone.

The animals peeked at her. Leilani's reaction was the best one of all. She did a double take at the sight of Boo and then tried to back away from the stall door as quickly as possible, all while making a screeching sound like she had seen a ghost.

His name matched, then.

Alarmed, Chelsie stopped sweeping Velvet's stall and poked her head out to see what was happening. Her eyes went wide like galaxies when she saw Boo.

Carolina put him on the floor, and several things happened at once.

First, Luna streaked down from her spot in the rafters and started swiping at Carolina's ankles. For a second the surprise was so great, Carolina laughed. The cat had only done that to Chelsie, and Caro had been secretly jealous. But then Luna changed tactics and employed claws. They went through the heavy socks and fleece pants Carolina was wearing, scratching her skin.

"Ouch, Luna!" She tried not to scream so as not to spook the horses or the puppy. But it took a lot of self-control because her ankle burned with pain.

Chelsie had darted into the aisle to fend Luna off, but Boo had started chasing the cat, so Chelsie had gone after him instead. Which in turn made him run even more.

And then Twinkletoes made such a high-pitched braying sound that it froze the girls, cat, dog, and every creature within a two-mile radius. Carolina could almost translate it into human speech. "Stranger danger!"

It was a scream meant to scare a predator.

The dog.

It was almost comical how Twinks stood his ground at the door of the stall he shared with Bella—if they hadn't been so anxious. The whites of Bella's eyes were large, which showed how scared she was. And Twinkletoes was protecting her. It wouldn't be right to laugh at their feelings.

Carolina's heart about melted like sugar in water.

"I guess bringing Boo to the barn isn't at the top of ideas I've ever had."

Chelsie shook her head and raised her eyebrows. "Really? In my opinion it's really high up—the list of bad ideas." But she grinned at Carolina, who exhaled in relief.

She had thought Boo would laze around like he had at the cottage, not become a barking machine. What had happened to the sweet puppy who didn't make a sound?

Carolina and Chelsie tried to speak, but it was impossible with the racket. The only way Boo would stay quiet was if Carolina picked him up. If not, his haunches lifted, and he'd go back to barking at the horses.

"Caro . . ." Chelsie managed to say. "He really needs a leash."

Carolina's heart fell all the way to the center of the magma of the earth.

Papi had brought Boo home with the intention of taking him on trail rides. But if Boo attacked their own horses, then that would be impossible. And really, what kind of farm dog would he be? He was a working dog. They couldn't keep him at the cottage if he wasn't going to do his part to keep Paradise in business.

The money from the trail rides would help cover the

expenses the sponsors didn't. No trail rides, no more scholar-ships. Without scholarships, Unbridled Dreams would become just another exclusive program most people wouldn't have access to. Then all the work would've been for nothing . . .

Carolina was in a downward spiral of negative thoughts.

"I'm sorry! I don't know what got into him," she said as she tried to sweep with one hand while she held Boo with the other.

Besides becoming a Tasmanian devil, had he also doubled his body weight? He was so wiggly, Carolina couldn't really hold him and do chores at the same time.

"Why don't you take him up to your house for now?" Chelsie asked, clearly trying to be gentle.

Carolina shook her head. "I can't let you do all the chores by your—" She caught Boo just in time before he wiggled out of her arms and fell to the floor.

She sighed, knowing the more frustrated she became, the more the puppy wiggled, trying to get away from her. His previous trauma was causing him to make irrational decisions.

"Here," Chelsie said, coming over with a piece of rope. "Let me see if this can double as a leash at least until you get him back to the house. He's too large to be carried like a baby, and if you take him out, he might dart off and get lost in the storm."

The images her words sparked in Carolina's mind were terrifying.

Boo lost in the woods. Boo howling with cold. Boo coming across a pack of hungry coyotes. She shivered.

"You're right," she said.

"We'll stop by to drive you to school, okay? You're going to miss the bus," Chelsie said.

Chelsie usually rode in the car with her mom while Carolina insisted on riding the bus. She was fanatical about keeping some boundaries. Just because they lived on the same property didn't mean they had to do everything together. Chelsie shared some alone time with her mom, and Carolina got to catch up with Vida.

She wanted to say no thank you to the invitation, but a glance at the clock told her that she was cutting it close. And then she glanced at her clothes and saw them covered with hair, drool, and mud. Where had the mud come from when she'd carried Boo the whole way?

She wasn't a fashionista like Chelsie and Vida, but that didn't mean she was going to show up to school looking like a scarecrow left out for the whole winter. She was definitely going to miss the bus.

"Okay," she said, and then she remembered her manners. "Thank you, Chels. I owe you big-time."

Chelsie smiled and shrugged like it was nothing, but to Carolina, her friendship and support meant the world. "That's why we're a good team."

"I'll make it up to you!" Carolina promised as she headed out, leading the dog with the makeshift leash.

"You better!" she heard from inside the barn.

The music started again, and Carolina could practically hear the animals' relief that she was taking Boo with her.

Luna sat at the door and hissed at them as they walked out.

"Wow, Luna," Carolina said. "That's harsh, even from you."

Boo followed her at the beginning of their trek uphill, but halfway back to the little cottage he planted his bum on the freezing gravel and refused to move. She had to pick him up so they wouldn't turn into a modern sculpture of snow and ice.

By the time Carolina got inside, she was sure even a scarecrow left out all winter would be laughing at her.

Her mom took a look at her. Something flashed in her eyes, and Carolina inwardly begged her not to say anything.

Mom kept her lips sealed and took Boo from her hands. "How about I keep him in the laundry room for now?"

Carolina sighed. She was equal parts relieved her mom was helping and frustrated that Boo would be locked in a room.

"Just until he learns the rules of his new family. Caro, it's imperative that he learn right from the beginning if we want to avoid bigger problems in the future, okay?"

"Okay," she said, trying to ignore Boo's big, innocent puppy eyes.

"Now, go change so you can make it to school," Mom said.

Carolina climbed the stairs three steps at a time. It wasn't even seven thirty and she was already exhausted.

11

No One's Favorite

On the ride to school, Carolina almost fell asleep. This had never happened before.

"Do you need me to drive you back home?" Heather asked, sounding concerned as she glanced in the rearview mirror.

Chelsie placed a hand on Carolina's forehead, but her temperature must have been fine because she didn't say anything.

Carolina knew she didn't have a fever. She was just sleep deprived.

"It's okay, Heather. Thank you though," she replied.

But maybe she should've accepted the offer to go back home. The whole morning was like a bizarre dream. Vida had to talk to one of her teachers during lunchtime, and Carolina wasn't able to speak with Gisella either. She'd seen a glimpse of her on her way back from lunch, but everyone had inside recess, so she couldn't talk to her after all.

Carolina came home to find her mom had gone shopping and had brought home supplies for the new dog. Most importantly, a crate.

"I don't want to leave him here all day, Mom," Carolina whined. "He must be lonely."

Boo had been quiet the whole time Carolina had been back home, but she didn't need to hear him whimpering to know he was scared. His whole body language said *fear*.

Papi, home for a break, overheard her and came into the kitchen. "Now, Caro," he said. "Think about how a horse would feel if you left him roaming free in a barn. No stalls. No little room for him to retreat to when he needs some peace and quiet. Or left him out in the pasture with no refuge from the weather or place to collect his thoughts. How would he feel?"

Carolina rolled her eyes. "But Boo isn't a horse, Papi. He's a dog, little reminder."

Papi ruffled her hair and said, "Horses and dogs are not that different."

"Horses are prey and dogs are predators," Carolina countered. "They're worlds apart."

Papi insisted, "That's true, but their behavior is very similar. At least, the way you train them is very similar. They all need structure, just like children. So now help me put this gate together to keep your Boo out of the kitchen."

Carolina wasn't happy to add another boundary for her puppy, but she complied. Mainly because she always loved building things with her dad. At the end, she was happy with how the gate turned out, although like always, they ended up with a lot of extra pieces.

"Are we missing something?" she asked, perplexed. They'd followed all the instructions.

"It's better that we have leftovers instead of going without," Mom said.

There she was, always seeing the bright side of things. Carolina made an effort to be more grateful with her parents.

Boo wasn't a horse, but he was the first animal that was solely hers. And she needed help.

That night at her lesson, she asked to ride Pepino, but Kimber insisted she take Shadow instead.

"Just because things are hard, it doesn't mean you have to give up," the trainer said.

Maybe Shadow was tired of fighting too, because even though he still refused to give her one of the join-up hugs Carolina had seen him give Chelsie and Kimber, at least he walked in her direction at the end of their groundwork. Before he changed his mind, she climbed in the saddle. They'd taken a couple of turns around the arena when she saw Chelsie walk in beside Gisella, who was leading Leilani, the chestnut quarter horse. Tessa and Loretta followed closely behind.

Gisella's lesson was today? Carolina had been so preoccupied with Boo, and so sleep deprived, she'd lost track of the days of the week.

Gisella didn't seem like she would need Carolina around for her lesson, since she already had so much help, but the surprise woke Carolina up quickly. Shadow seemed to sense her mind was elsewhere because he tried to switch directions. Carolina lost her balance, but instead of giving loud voice commands, she held on to the saddle, tightening her legs around Shadow's girth and pushing her heels deep into the stirrups.

"Good job!" Kimber cheered from the center of the arena.

At least Kimber had complimented her in front of everyone.

Carolina glanced at the group of girls again to see their reactions. Gisella wore a Velvet Lilly sweatshirt and had her hair in French braids. She looked just like Chelsie—and Tessa and Loretta, for that matter.

Maybe they'd coordinated on matching today?

Any grogginess still clinging to Carolina left her like a sigh. She hadn't gotten the memo on what to wear. But honestly, if she had, she wouldn't have worn a Velvet Lilly hoodie anyway. She didn't own one. Besides, she didn't know how to French braid her hair, and now she wouldn't ask Chelsie or anyone else to teach her how. She didn't want to appear desperate to fit in when all her life she'd been okay sporting her unique style, as her mom said. *Unique* sounded like code for unfashionable.

Her cheeks felt hot, and her armpits prickled with sweat.

Although it seemed obvious that Gisella preferred Cheslie to her, at least the new girl was making friends in Unbridled Dreams. Carolina didn't have to be everyone's favorite. Still, it hurt a little.

Loretta and Tessa headed to the big barn, to get their horses, most likely. Carolina took her chance to bridge the distance with the new girl.

"Hi, Gi!" she called.

Gisella looked up from something Chelsie was showing her on her phone and gave Carolina a fleeting smile and a nod.

While Carolina finished her lesson with Shadow, Chelsie and Gisella spoke in Spanish on the sideline. Carolina tried to catch what they were saying. She caught snatches of conversation about their classes and the weather, and the last Velvet Lilly song that had *dropped*, whatever that meant, the week before. There were a few *chéveres* and *chamas* thrown around, and Carolina made a mental note to ask her dad what those words meant. What kind of Latina was she?

As she and Shadow circled the arena, Carolina's brain was

searching for the right words to say in Spanish as soon as she was out of the saddle. But her mind went blank as she tried to translate what she really wanted to say: that she was glad to see Gisella. That she wanted to be friends even if their musical tastes were different. After all, Vida loved crafts, which were torture for Carolina, but they still got along grandly.

But after she hurriedly dismounted and gave a half-hearted pat on the flank to Shadow, all she said to Gisella, in English, was "Have you been watching the videos that I sent you?" She wanted to talk about Gisella's riding . . . but did it come out sounding like Carolina was a teacher checking up on Gisella's homework?

Gisella's cheeks blushed bright red like holly berries. So . . . maybe.

"Watch them when you have time, Gise," Chelsie said in a soothing voice, and Gisella smiled gratefully at her.

"I've been trying to catch up with homework. I'm sorry."

A knot grew in Carolina's throat. She should've known Gisella had other things in her life competing for her time. After all, just because she was in Unbridled Dreams, it didn't mean that she had to be obsessed with horses like Carolina was. She just loved the videos she'd sent to Gisella, and was sure they would help her prep for her lessons.

Carolina didn't know how to break through the oppressive silence that had fallen on them. But luckily, someone completely unexpected ran into the arena.

"Vida!" Carolina exclaimed. She handed Shadow's reins to Chelsie and ran to greet her friend. Someone who loved her unconditionally! Her oldest and dearest friend. "What are you doing here?"

Vida shrugged, the purple tips of her hair brushing her shoulders. "I signed up to read to Bella with my little buddy, but she isn't here yet. I figured I'd say hi to you in the meantime. Maybe I can see Boo?"

Vida wasn't a horse person, but little by little, she was warming up to them. Coming to read to the horses was a big step. On the other hand, she loved dogs and couldn't get enough of Caro's new puppy.

"Did you take your allergy medicine?"

Vida's eyes and nose usually started running as soon as she

stepped onto Paradise Ranch. Or any ranch for that matter. She was sensitive to hay and horsehair. Carolina shuddered thinking about how lucky she was that she didn't have to worry about sneezing every time she was next to her animal friends.

"Of course," Vida said, and then her eyes landed on Gisella and Chelsie, who were standing in the middle of the arena. Kimber was off to one side talking on her phone.

"Hey, Chelsie! Hi, Gisella," Vida said.

"Hi, Vida," Chelsie and Gisella said in unison.

"I'm glad you're part of Unbridled Dreams now, Gisella!"

"You're taking lessons too?" Gisella asked, her eyes twinkling as she spoke to Carolina's best friend as if they'd known each other forever.

Vida grimaced and her eyes flitted in Carolina's direction. "I like horses, but I'm actually a little allergic." As if on cue, she sneezed.

After a chorus of *Bless you* and *¡Salud!,* Vida added, "And I'm also a little scared of them."

Carolina rolled her eyes. Not this again.

"So am I!" Gisella exclaimed as if, finally, someone understood how she felt.

"Why are you scared of them?" Vida asked. Carolina wouldn't have thought to ask. What good reason was there for being scared of them? "For me, it started when I was in kindergarten and we went to this summer carnival, and a pony chewed my hair!"

Gisella clasped her hands over her mouth. "Back in Venezuela, I saw a horse step on a man's foot and break it. I'm a dancer. What if that ever happened to me?" She turned to look at Leilani. The mare was considerably taller and bigger than Pepino, whom Gisella had ridden last time.

"I used to be terrified of my dad's horse, Paraná," Chelsie chimed in. "I'm still a little scared of him."

Carolina wanted to stop this conversation. She didn't want them to bond over what could go wrong with a horse. But she didn't know how to redirect them.

Fortunately, Kimber was done with her call.

"Ready for your lesson, Gisella?" she asked in Spanish.

Gisella bit her lip nervously but nodded.

"I have to go," she said and walked over to the trainer with Leilani.

"See you later," Carolina said, scrambling to find the right words that would reassure Gisella. She couldn't come up with anything fast enough in Spanish, so she said in English, "Remember, if you need any help or you have any questions, come to me. You know I—"

"I know you know everything about horses. I got it," Gisella said.

The words froze the smile on Carolina's face. She wouldn't say she knew *everything* about horses, but she knew some things. All she'd done was offer her help, but something in Gisella's body language told her the other girl hadn't necessarily been complimenting her.

Maybe *next* time Carolina wouldn't put her foot in her mouth.

She'd intended to stay and watch Gisella's lesson, but Vida asked, "Can we go see Boo?"

"I have to put Shadow away," she said.

"I'll do it," Chelsie offered. "You go home with Vida."

Carolina was torn. Gisella was doing well during ground-work, and she wanted to see how everything went. But she couldn't say no to either of her friends. She headed out, leaving just as Gisella scrambled away from Leilani when the quarter horse tried to lean her head on the girl's shoulder. Caro almost went back, but Kimber was right there, along with Chelsie, Loretta, and Tessa. They were all cheering for Gisella.

Carolina knew when she wasn't needed.

· U ·

Later that night, after Vida had gone home, she and Chelsie met to say good night to Velvet.

"Did Gisella's lesson go well?" she asked, her eyes fixed on the same spot of floor she'd been sweeping for the last five minutes.

Chelsie sighed. "She was a little spooked, you know what I mean?"

"Leilani?"

"Gisella," Chelsie replied, gently taking the broom from Caro's hand and carefully placing it on its hook by the door.

"Next Wednesday I'll stay to watch the whole thing," Carolina said with determination. "I know I can help."

Chelsie shook her head. "She changed her lesson time to Friday."

On Friday, Carolina would be volunteering with the reading program winners, and she wouldn't get to see Gisella at her riding lesson. Again. One more bummer added to her rotten couple of weeks.

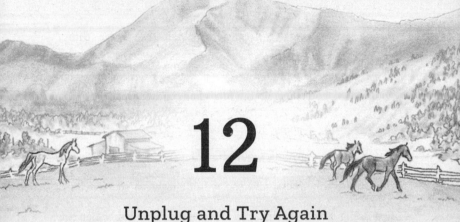

12

Unplug and Try Again

The next three Fridays, Carolina would hurry to finish her chores and her responsibilities with the library patrons who had earned time with the horses, but she was always too late to even catch a few minutes of Gisella's class.

Chelsie and Kimber assured Carolina that even without her help, Gisella was advancing as expected. Maybe she wouldn't become the horsewoman Carolina aspired to be, but she was having a good experience at Unbridled Dreams.

A good enough experience won't be enough for Gisella to write a glowing review of the program, Carolina thought.

She couldn't stop worrying about the future of this project that meant so much to her.

But yesterday at school, when her teacher had asked her to drop off a message with the librarian, she'd taken a turn down the fourth-grade hallway. The walls had been decorated with posters about the students' favorite animals. There were pandas, lions, dogs, and cats. A fluffy cow made her smile. But when she came upon the poster of an Arabian horse that looked very much like Shadow, she found the name Gisella Bassi printed neatly in a bottom corner. Carolina's heart about burst with joy.

This had to be a sign that even if she and Gisella hadn't become best friends, at least the new girl hadn't had a horrible experience at Paradise, right?

The one who seemed to love life the best at the ranch, though, was Boo.

He wasn't waking up so much during the night anymore.

Carolina was getting better at not only telling him what to do but also listening to what he wanted to say. It wasn't easy, but she loved him. And because she loved him, stopping to listen to his body language became a fun challenge for her. And him.

But Shadow was another story.

Her lesson with him last night had been more of the same. She had—mostly—stopped giving him verbal commands when they did groundwork to avoid falling into the trap of sending mixed messages, like Kimber had warned her. She made sure she was giving him all the physical clues for him to trust her, but Shadow still didn't seem to be listening to her.

In fact, their relationship was worse than ever. Now his only two gaits were walk or trot. For the last couple of lessons Carolina had with Kimber, he wouldn't switch into a canter no matter how she asked.

"Maybe unplug for a little bit," Kimber had suggested yesterday when Caro had dismounted from Shadow, defeated and discouraged.

"Unplug?" she asked, confused. "I'm never on electronics."

Her mom gave her this advice plenty, but it was only after she'd spent too much time watching YouTube videos.

"I mean, take a break," Kimber said as she took Shadow's reins. "Literally. Tomorrow after school, before you come down to the barn, take a nap and reset."

Carolina didn't know how that would help, but she was

desperate for any kind of trick that would help her unlock the mystery of Shadow not clicking with her.

And this afternoon, when she woke up, she was surprised by how refreshed she felt. She rubbed the nap from her eyes and walked across her room to the window. It had snowed again, or rather, it hadn't stopped snowing all week. After she washed her face, she headed downstairs, curious about how quiet the cottage was. She found a note on the table that read *I took Boo out for a walk to the big barn.*

It was her dad's handwriting.

Her first impulse was to run out and meet them. Although he'd already been at Paradise for a few weeks, Boo hadn't been to the big barn yet.

Carolina didn't want to miss Boo's first time meeting the big horses. They wouldn't react like Twinkletoes had, would they? But even if they did, her dad would be there supervising everything. She trusted him.

She looked at the time and went over the schedule for the evening. Kimber would still be teaching, and Chelsie would be doing the little barn chores.

She decided to go down and help her.

She bundled up and left the cottage, wishing she'd had the presence of mind to eat something before she dashed out.

The little barn was immaculately clean already, and the horses and donkey warm and comfy in their stalls. The only empty one was Velvet's. Like always, Carolina felt a rush of longing that Chelsie and Velvet had each other. When would she find the horse of her heart?

She kissed her ponies and Twinks and headed for the indoor arena. Maybe she'd have a chance to ride Velvet after Chelsie was done with her lesson.

The wind and snow prickled her face, and she was happy to arrive in the shelter of the arena. Shadow was tied to the patience post in a corner. Carolina nodded at him when she passed him. "What trouble did you get into?"

He snorted and looked away. Couldn't they have a simple conversation?

To her surprise, Boo was sitting at Gisella's feet in the stands, all curled up like a cat.

Gisella was stroking his fur and he obviously loved the

attention. Carolina wanted to come up with something funny or clever to say, but no words came to mind—in Spanish or English. Or actually, they all sounded a little aggressive, like: *How come you're here on a Thursday?* or *Why aren't you riding?* or *Why are you with my dog?*

Tessa had just galloped around the arena under Kimber's supervision in perfect form. She never once lifted her knees when Apollo, her horse, broke into a gallop. Maybe it was because her horse knew her and trusted her? Well, or because she trusted Apollo. Tessa had only had him for a few months, but they were already so synchronized. It was a beauty to see how Tessa didn't even have to make a verbal command, but she was obviously telling him something that he understood right away. How did she do it?

Carolina bit her lip as she remembered how Shadow ignored her signals.

She was doing everything right, but Shadow just didn't listen to her. He wanted to take charge, but she was the leader. She was the one who was supposed to tell him what to do and when.

But she didn't know how to do it. He was too stubborn. Too powerful.

Maybe she should give up and be happy to accept that, with Shadow, she'd never be vulnerable enough to let him take the lead. She did perfectly well on any other horse. Why did it matter so much to her to force things to work with Shadow?

Tessa brought Apollo to a perfect halt, and there was a burst of clapping. Carolina was surprised that while she'd been overanalyzing her relationship with Shadow, the other girls had joined Gisella.

"Caro!" Chelsie waved her over to the edge of the arena.

Boo awoke at the noise. When he saw her, the puppy bounded toward her, wagging his tail.

"Oh, hi, sweetheart. Did you miss me?" She crouched down so he could lick her face. Then he heeled her when she headed toward Chelsie.

"We're waiting for Tessa to be done," Chelsie explained, "and then Gisella is going to try riding shapes with Velvet."

"But her class is on Friday," Carolina said.

"She needed to ride with Tessa, so Kimber said it was okay to change to today."

Carolina felt like nothing ever went the way she wanted. "Really? I wanted to ride Velvet. Gisella can ride . . ." She looked around as if there was a line of horses waiting to volunteer for the job, but the only one was Shadow.

Surly, bad-humored Shadow.

"You can ride Shadow," she said, remembering the idea she'd had a while back. Shadow liked to take the lead. Gisella was afraid of taking charge. They were the perfect match!

Loretta rolled her eyes and muttered something at Gisella, whose cheeks blushed. She looked at Boo, avoiding looking at Carolina.

"What, Loretta?" Carolina asked. "What did you tell her?"

It was obvious that Gisella's English was getting better if she was gossiping with Loretta. And not even behind Carolina's back.

"I only said that we were having fun until you showed up," Loretta said defiantly. It was so weird how she and Bracken had the same face, but their expressions were so different when they looked at Carolina.

"Lori!" Chelsie said. "Don't be mean."

"It's okay," Carolina said, lifting her chin. "My dad always says that for silly words, the best is not to hear, so there."

"You don't listen to anyone to begin with. That's the real problem," Loretta mumbled.

Carolina clenched her teeth so she wouldn't lash out further at Loretta. She always knew what to say to get Caro all riled up. She wasn't going to fall for it now. She kept her eyes on the arena, wishing for a moment she could go back to those good ole days when she'd been the only kid at the ranch.

But no. That's not really what she wanted. How long had she wished for other kids to be at the property? Now that this wish had been granted, she'd just have to deal with the consequences. Next time, she'd have to be more specific with what she asked for.

Tessa was done, and she rode Apollo on a leisurely walk around the arena. Kimber had helped her take her boots and socks off, and Tessa had let the reins drop so Apollo would walk slowly.

Eager to talk to Kimber, Caro looked at Boo and said, "Stay here. I'll be back soon."

She walked to where the trainer was watching Tessa and Apollo, clearly pleased and proud.

To Caro's surprise, Boo obeyed her. Carolina would've done cartwheels across the arena if she'd known how.

"Hey, Caro," Kimber said, smiling.

Carolina wrung her hands, but she asked, "Is it okay if today I ride Velvet? I was already planning to." Before Kimber interrupted her, she added, "Gisella can ride Shadow. I think he'd be good for her. I really do."

Kimber's eyes went from her to Gisella, then to Velvet, and then to Shadow. Finally, she nodded and said, "I see what you mean. I think it's a good match."

Now Carolina jumped for joy. "Yay! Thank you, Kimber." Before she ran to Velvet, she couldn't help herself. She gave Kimber a tight hug.

13

Honey, Not Vinegar

Buoyed by her joy, Carolina channeled all her confidence into groundwork with Velvet, who didn't hesitate to join up.

She kept to one end of the arena while Tessa led Apollo to the big barn to put him away for the night. Loretta went with them, and Carolina breathed a sigh of relief.

Chelsie stayed with Boo, who sat obediently by her side.

Carolina mounted Velvet and soon was galloping the perimeter of the arena with the mare, until she fell into a trance and her breathing calmed and she imagined they were running outside in the woods. From the corner of her eye, she saw that Shadow and Gisella were getting along great, and she felt a surge of satisfaction that she had suggested the pairing.

By the time she went to dismount, her cheeks kind of hurt. She was smiling for the first time in what felt like weeks.

Boo, excited that she was done with Velvet, started barking. Chelsie shortened his leash and crouched down to talk to him.

Velvet began nervously stepping in place, but Carolina touched her neck gently. "Shhh."

And then she sent Boo a look.

Boo made such a funny expression that Carolina couldn't help laughing.

Carolina got off the horse, but Boo still sat, waiting patiently next to Chelsie. He was such a good dog!

"Thanks for watching him for me."

"Of course," Chelsie said, ruffling Boo's fur. "Thanks for warming up Velvet for me."

Pleased that Boo and Chelsie had clicked, Carolina thanked Velvet and Chelsie for the ride. She was about to take Boo back to the house when Gisella called out to her. "Wait!" She had just hopped off Shadow.

The younger girl ran in her direction. And Carolina's soul soared.

But Gisella said, "I wanted to say good night to Boo."

She knelt down and kissed the dog on the forehead. Boo covered her face with kisses. Carolina reminded herself that love wasn't a pie that ran out of pieces. The more you show it to others, the more love grows.

She might not speak Spanish, or like Velvet Lilly, and Gisella might never love horses the way Carolina did, but perhaps Boo could help them bridge their differences?

"Do you want me to help you clean up Shadow?" she asked tentatively.

Gisella smiled gratefully and Carolina's heart thumped. This was it. The moment that they'd become best friends.

But then Gisella's eyes flickered toward Chelsie and said, "Actually, Chelsie is going to help me. Is that okay?"

Carolina's hopes sank, but she smiled. "Of course. I'd be happy to help next time. But only if you need me. You're doing great."

Gisella's cheeks blushed a soft pink. Finally, she had said something right.

"Let's go, Boo," Carolina said.

But Boo had felt the slack leash and took his chance. The leash slipped through Carolina's fingers as he darted unexpectedly toward the middle of the arena. Carolina's breath caught as he began weaving between the legs of Velvet and Shadow, who stood frozen with fear.

Carolina didn't think.

She chased him. But the faster she ran, the faster Boo ran too. Soon, running on the soft footing of the arena exhausted her, and she was panting, out of breath. When Carolina stopped, clutching a stitch in her side, Boo made as if he was willingly coming to her. But when she tried to step on the leash, he ran between her legs.

Gisella, Chelsie, and Kimber watched her, and she was so embarrassed she could've cried. But that would have only made matters worse.

"Boo," Gisella called in a high-pitched, sweet voice. "Come here."

And at once, Boo stopped running, his ears perked up. She knelt, patting her leg, and called one more time, and he ran to Gisella.

Carolina was shocked into silence.

Was that all it took for Boo to be obedient? Just a call?

Carolina trudged over to Gisella and said, "Thank you. How did you do that?"

Gisella cuddled Boo up to her face, whispering to him. Then she looked up at Carolina and said in Spanish, "My mom always says it's easier to attract with honey than vinegar."

Chelsie and Kimber both had sympathetic looks on their faces, but Carolina was drowning in embarrassment anyway. She was supposed to be one of the leaders of Unbridled Dreams, but here she was causing extra trouble.

Without a word, she took Boo from Gisella's arms and headed out toward the cottage, cheeks burning.

14

A Trickster

The embarrassment lingered in the pit of Carolina's stomach for a couple of weeks. Her only consolation was hearing from Chelsie and Kimber that Gisella and Shadow were becoming a wonderful team. Caro had to see it with her own eyes.

One day while doing chores, Carolina saw in the schedule that Gisella was supposed to start trotting that week.

The sting in her wounded ego had finally dulled enough for her to show up at Gisella's lesson. Carolina walked into the arena with Boo—leashed—just as Chelsie was starting a practice with Velvet. Caro kept close to the wall on her way to the stands in the corner, and was happy to see Boo didn't even flick an ear at the mare. She'd been extra careful with him, and he was doing much better at being around the horses. Mom had made him a tiny sweater with the Unbridled Dreams logo. Carolina asked for it to be purple. It was Gisella's favorite color after all.

Carolina made sure to wear a purple hoodie too and was happy to see that, without coordinating, Chelsie was matching.

"That color looks good on you, Boo," Chelsie said. "And you too, Caro."

Caro smiled, and then she asked, "Do you think I should get Shadow tacked for Gisella? That way she'll have more time for riding when she arrives."

Chelsie considered, but then she shook her head. "She likes doing it herself."

"You're right," Caro agreed. "And she does a good job at it."

"She sure does," Chelsie said.

Carolina tried to wait patiently. It was hard for her though. Chelsie trotted around with Velvet, while Caro and Boo watched them from the bleachers, waiting for Gisella to arrive.

The beating of Velvet's hooves on the soft footing seemed

to count down the minutes, and when Caro looked up at the clock by the entrance, she realized the time for the lesson had come and gone, and still there was no sign of Gisella.

Kimber peeked in, then led in Shadow, who was all tacked up. After tethering him to a post, the trainer walked back out before Carolina could ask if something had happened with their student.

Boo had fallen asleep, so unable to contain her impatience, Carolina secured the leash around the metal frame of the bleachers and walked out to the entrance. The day was sunny and a little windy, but still cold. She looked at the road. There were no cars in sight.

She went back inside just when Chelsie was bringing Velvet to a halt and dismounted.

"Do you think she's sick?" Carolina asked.

In Caro's mind, the only reason someone would miss a class with Kimber was if they were super ill.

Even if she were on her deathbed, she'd do anything to make it to class with Kimber.

Boo woke up and whined. Carolina untied the leash.

"Aw, are you getting bored, Boo?" Chelsie asked, before she unlatched the cinch around Velvet's girth. Standing on the mounting block, she lifted the saddle off the mare's back with an "oof" of effort.

Carolina went into the arena to give her a hand, and together they placed the saddle on the ground. Boo had followed Carolina, and now he circled the girls, the blue leash trailing behind him, as if wondering how he could help.

"You're a good, good boy." Carolina always tried to speak to him in that voice Gisella had used with him, and it had been working.

When she spoke sternly to him, it was like he forgot all his training. Like he was too scared to think. But when she was sweet, even if the sweetness bordered on saccharine, he tried his best to do what she asked.

Wanting to show off his new skills to Chelsie, Carolina said, "Look at this, Chels. Boo, sit." She made sure to keep her voice sweet as honey. He was so adorable, she didn't even have to fake it at all.

He sat obediently. He'd stay there until she told him he could move.

"Good boy!" Chelsie said and clapped.

He looked up at her and offered a paw. Carolina shook it, but he looked sad.

"He wants a treat," Chelsie said, rummaging in her pocket for something. She offered him a piece of something she found, and he gobbled it up.

"Don't look at me that way," Chelsie said.

"I didn't say anything," Carolina replied.

"You don't need to. I know that look and you're wondering what I fed him." Chelsie gave Boo another piece of what looked like . . . apple chips?

Carolina smiled, relieved. "You walk around with apple chips in the pockets of your jacket?"

Chelsie shrugged and turned out her pockets. A rain of crumbs fell on the ground, and quickly, Boo licked up every little bit.

"I had some apple chips for Velvet, and I thought he'd like them too."

Boo came up to Carolina and lifted his paw. By the look on his face, now she could see he wasn't trying to shake hands but that he was begging for food!

"I have a carrot," she said, and then she looked at Chelsie. "Do you think dogs eat carrots too?"

Chelsie shrugged. "As long as it's not chocolate, he can eat anything. At least that's what Gisella said the other day."

"Speaking of Gisella, where could she be? I don't understand how she can be late," she said. "If I were her—"

"But you are you and Gisella is Gisella," Chelsie interrupted her.

In that moment, Velvet rolled on the arena ground like a big puppy and Boo joined her from a safe distance.

"Oh, Velvet!" Carolina exclaimed.

For a second, the two girls watched horse and dog with the pride of two mamas.

It was good to see Velvet make her own fun.

Spring shows were just around the corner and Velvet had a lot of work to do, but she also had come a long way.

Carolina's chest warmed with happiness.

Velvet's leg had healed completely and, more importantly, her trust in people had grown, particularly in Chelsie, who was her main rider. In fact, they had connected so much these last few weeks that she and Velvet seemed like two halves of the same creature. Carolina was getting better about acknowledging her jealousy of the relationship they had, but setting it aside so she could feel sheer joy for them.

She liked to tease Chelsie about the competition outfits and the rigid rules of the sport, but she really admired her friend. Although she wasn't interested in equitation competitions, she admired those riders. She even respected the things Loretta and her horse, Poseidon, could do. Not that she'd ever say it aloud.

Shadow snorted and pawed at the arena footing.

"Oh, Shadow!" Chelsie said.

Carolina rolled her eyes at him, but she couldn't stay mad at any of the animals at the ranch for long. Not even him.

Shadow had seemed eager as he walked into the arena with Kimber. But as the clock ticked on, unforgiving, he continued to paw at the ground impatiently. Chelsie got Velvet groomed and put away and still there was no sign of Gisella.

It was a waste of a tacked-up horse, in Carolina's opinion.

Apparently, Chelsie thought so too, because when she got back to the stands, she said, "Just take poor Shadow out of his misery. Can't you see he's bursting to go on a ride?"

Carolina eyed Shadow with a mixture of resentment and misgivings. But she gave in, of course, because she'd never said no to a chance to ride.

"I guess I'll sacrifice myself," Caro said teasingly. She grabbed a helmet and looked at Boo. "You stay here, okay, baby?"

"He'll stay with me," Chelsie said. "Don't worry."

Boo sat at Chelsie's feet.

Carolina headed toward Shadow. His side-eye seemed to challenge her.

She smirked. "You think you're so tough," she said. "But I'm tougher, sir."

As if he understood her words, Shadow nickered. He stomped his hoof, impatient to start. And although a part of her wanted to go on a fast gallop too, she was more concerned about making sure he understood *she* was still the one in charge.

Not willing to go through the humiliation of being rejected, she didn't do a join-up, not even a halfhearted one. This change of routine confused Shadow. He seemed perplexed that they were skipping groundwork, but surprisingly, shockingly, when she walked to the mounting block, he followed her with his head lowered, submissive.

"Was not playing your games the way to your heart, you big bully?" she teased him. "Maybe we should change things up more around here. What do you say?"

Before mounting, Carolina checked Shadow's girth and let down the stirrups. Although Gisella was younger, she was taller than Carolina. Since Gisella had been the last one in this saddle, Shadow waited obediently for Carolina to shorten the stirrups. Then she got in the saddle and settled in her seat. She did a reins check, and Shadow turned his head every time she asked for it, then turned in circles this way and that.

For the first time, it felt like the two of them were collaborating and, most importantly, communicating. She tried not to get too excited.

He walked next to the edge of the arena patiently. Boo had curled into a crescent and gone to sleep.

When she was satisfied Shadow was following her directions, Carolina kissed her lips and he started trotting. Instinctively, she started posting, rhythmically rising and falling as she followed the dance and the music of his hooves on the arena's footing.

The engine of a car sounded in the distance as if it was driving toward the ranch, but Carolina ignored it, pressing her heels down. It was easy to get into a trance when she connected with a horse this way. Shadow's ears remained pricked forward.

If only things always worked like this between them, the two of them could have so much fun!

And then without warning, Shadow took off in a mad dash of a gallop.

What a trickster! Carolina felt like her stomach had been left behind in his dust.

"Whoa!" she exclaimed before she could stop her words. Instead of slowing down, he gathered up explosive speed.

She saw the blur of Chelsie standing up, and heard her friend's panicked voice telling her to hold on and sit back. But in her surprise, her reins had fallen. She was only holding on to the horn of the saddle. And before she could prepare herself, Shadow skidded to a stop.

Carolina went flying.

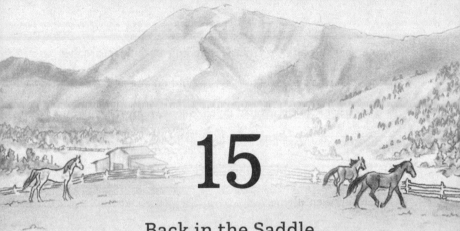

15

Back in the Saddle

Next thing she knew, Carolina was on the ground, looking at the beams crisscrossing the ceiling. Her first thought was *Good thing I was wearing a helmet!*

Boo barked, but someone's voice soothed him.

"Ouch," she said, rolling to her side to see who'd stopped him from running toward her.

Chelsie had Shadow's reins so he wouldn't trample Carolina or take off again. But there was no need. It was very classic that he had stopped running as soon as his rider fell. He just stood there. As did Boo, right next to Gisella, who watched the whole thing with a panic-stricken expression.

Carolina rolled back, facing up, feeling her heart slowing

into a more normal tempo now that the adrenaline was drain-
ing from her body.

Ugh, Shadow! Why was he so stubborn? They'd been doing
so well.

She felt betrayed.

And why had Gisella seen the whole thing? When had she
even arrived? Carolina was dismayed.

The sound of footsteps rushing in her direction rumbled
like thunder inside her helmet. Andrew and JC, two of the
stable hands, and Kimber all appeared in Carolina's line of
vision, looking concerned.

"Stay down a moment," Kimber said.

"I'm fine," Carolina said.

JC put three fingers in front of her and asked, "How many
fingers do you see?"

She debated whether or not to trick him, but then realized
this wasn't the moment to play pranks on anyone.

"Tres," she said.

"That's our girl," Andrew said, blue eyes sparkling with
relief, and offered his hand to help her get up on her feet.

Carolina gingerly got up, taking stock of her injuries. The greatest wound was to her ego.

She brushed the sawdust off her clothes and sent Shadow a poisonous look. "You and I are done," she said.

Andrew and JC laughed, maybe thinking she was joking. After all, this was Carolina Aguasvivas, the fearless girl with the magic touch.

Well, she thought, *not this time*.

This particular horse detested her, and she could've cried.

"It's okay, Caro," Kimber said. "As long as no one is hurt . . . Good thing you were wearing a helmet! What happened?"

She sighed, and without meeting Kimber's eyes, she confessed. "I got in the saddle without doing any groundwork. I'm sorry."

"Been there, done that," JC said, rubbing his behind as if he had painful memories.

"Well, missy, you know if you haven't fallen from a horse, it's only because you don't ride enough. Part of the job, right?" Andrew said.

Carolina nodded, but she glanced in Gisella's direction, hoping she hadn't heard what Andrew had just said.

Once everyone had made sure she was fine, JC and Andrew left to continue their jobs.

Falling from a horse wasn't the end of the world. But this kind of rejection from Shadow was really getting to her. Still, she was a leader, wasn't she? She couldn't walk away when things got hard.

"Do you want to get back on, at least for a short walk?" Kimber asked. "Don't end on a bad note tonight. But only if you feel safe, okay?"

Carolina wanted to do anything other than get back on, but she nodded. Kimber following a couple of steps behind, she headed to Shadow and took the reins from Chelsie's hand.

"Thanks for holding him," she said.

"Of course. Are you okay?" Chelsie's voice was heavy with concern.

But Carolina was more worried about what Gisella would think now than she was about herself.

Gisella had told Vida she was scared of horses after witnessing one step on a person's foot. Now seeing this, would she ever get back on Shadow? Gisella knelt a few steps away in the doorway to the aisle, whispering to Boo.

"I'm okay," Carolina said. "Come on, Shadow. Let's do some cooling down."

She stood next to him for a couple of heartbeats. He wasn't breathing hard, or acting like anything was bothering him.

"You could pretend to be a little sorry at least, you know?" she whispered, patting him. He was sweatier than she'd expected.

"Remember," Kimber said, "horses don't have the ability to pretend or act stubborn. With them, there's always a simple reason for why they act the way they do."

"Well," Carolina said. "He only throws a temper with me. Why?"

Kimber shrugged. "You're the most skilled rider he gets to spend time with."

This reply didn't help Carolina feel better at all.

"Are you okay?" Kimber asked again. "I can untack him and take him to his stall."

It was tempting, but she wasn't going to give in so easily.

"I want to get back on. Thanks," she said.

Kimber patted Shadow and went to talk to Gisella.

Gisella would have to ride Velvet now. Chelsie went to get the mare ready for another ride. Velvet wouldn't mind. She'd gotten to warm up with Chelsie.

Carolina's mind was a whirlwind of conflicting emotions as she overheard Gisella and Kimber's conversation. Gisella was late because Tessa had changed the time of her lesson, and Gisella didn't have a separate ride. Her parents had only one car.

"I'm sorry for being late," she said in a small voice.

"It's okay," Kimber replied. "I'm glad you're here. Are you okay riding Velvet?"

"If Chelsie's okay with it," Gisella replied.

Soon enough, Chelsie and Velvet were by Gisella's side.

Carolina turned back to the dappled gray Arabian beside

her. She could do what Kimber said and not end on a bad note, right? She wished that, instead, she could go back in time and sit back, press her heels down, convince Shadow not to break into that gallop. She'd long prided herself on knowing how to get things across to people and animals. Had she lost her magic?

Under Kimber's careful supervision, she got up on the saddle and walked Shadow one turn around the arena. He seemed like he didn't want to stop, but Carolina was done with him for the day. For a while, or forever even.

Why didn't he like her?

What did she have to do to get through to him?

As she rubbed him down in the aisle afterward, she looked into his eyes, trying to find the answer, but he averted his head.

She knew horses didn't like to be stared at, so she shouldn't take this personally. But she did.

She was tired of trying to do a simple thing with him and not being able to.

It had been a long time since she'd fallen off a horse.

Her ego and her bottom were sore.

Once she'd put Shadow away, she caught the end of Gisella's lesson. She looked great on Velvet. Caro stuck around until she could take Boo from Chelsie without interrupting everyone, and say goodbye to Gisella. The younger girl gave her a smile. "Maybe Shadow is trying to tell you something," she said shyly.

Carolina was taken aback. What would Gisella know about horses?

But she had known how to deal with Boo, hadn't she?

And hadn't Papi said that training horses was just like training dogs sometimes?

"Maybe," she said. Then she looked at Boo and said, "Let's go get you a treat, Boo. Good night, Gisella."

Shadow wanted to tell her something? If so, what was it? Why did he act up with her and not anyone else? He had an owner who boarded him at Paradise, but Kimber was using him as part of the lesson clinic because he'd been so gentle and nice with Loretta, some of the other new kids, and even Gisella, whose knowledge of horses and riding was just minimal.

As she left the barn with Boo beside her, she passed Shadow, who had walked out the back of his stall to the small attached paddock. Carolina turned away, frustrated and ready to be home.

But her heart prickled at her, so before starting up the hill, she looked over her shoulder and said, "Good night, Shadow." The Arabian snorted and stamped a back hoof in reply.

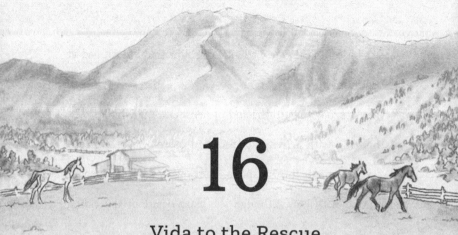

16

Vida to the Rescue

As the first session of Unbridled Dreams continued, Carolina couldn't be coaxed to ride Shadow anymore. She was glad she'd gotten back on him at the end of her lesson, but every time she approached his stall with a bucket of brushes, he eyed her with a challenge in his expression. She couldn't bear to put herself in a vulnerable situation again. For a while, Kimber tried to convince her, but eventually the trainer gave in and put Carolina on Velvet or Pepino. Once she even rode Leilani.

With Gisella, things weren't perfect, but at least the ice between her and Carolina had thawed a little after the day Carolina had fallen off the Arabian.

Still, they exchanged polite words here and there, but they

weren't becoming the best friends Carolina had envisioned at the beginning of the program.

One Saturday toward the end of February, the whole ranch was buzzing with activity. Chelsie had passed her advanced-rider requirements for the upcoming shows, and everyone was celebrating with her. Although she wasn't part of the riding clinic, Vida was invited to the little party Heather had prepared for right after Gisella's lesson. Before heading to the barn, Vida stopped by the cottage on the top of the hill.

Although she didn't show it, when Carolina opened the door for her friend, she felt like the sun had come out after a long winter. Like the birds and angels were singing. Like she was galloping through tall grasses on a perfectly behaved and respectful horse who adored her.

"You're not even ready yet?" Vida asked, dismayed, looking at her friend's outfit.

Carolina hadn't felt like celebrating. Too many concerns pulsed in her mind. But of course she'd be there for Chelsie's big accomplishment. She wasn't *that* kind of friend. However, she hadn't bothered to put on anything other than her usual dirt-stained jeans and black T-shirt.

When Carolina said, "Oh, I was still deciding what to wear," Vida saw right through the lie. She clicked her tongue and barged into the house and up the stairs to Caro's room, quickly followed by Carolina and Boo.

As soon as Boo walked into the room, he climbed on a chair and from there jumped into Caro's arms. Vida and Carolina laughed and laughed as he frantically kissed Caro's face. When he seemed satisfied, he wiggled out of her arms and headed to Vida.

"Oh, come here, you fluffball!" She knelt on the floor so he could kiss her too. But with her, he was a little more bashful. Only one kiss sufficed before he snuggled in the chair as if it were a throne.

"He's been shedding a little more than usual, so careful. His hair is hard to get off clothes," Carolina warned.

But Vida had already taken out a mini lint roller from her purse, which was shaped like a cat's face, and was carefully brushing her navy corduroy pants and bright yellow wool coat. Sensing that Carolina was staring at her, impressed, Vida said, "I came prepared." She took another mini roller from her purse and placed it on Caro's antique desk. *Antique* was code for old, ancient really, but Carolina loved this piece of furniture that once upon a time had belonged to Paradise's first one-room school.

Carolina was about to start rolling the brush on her clothes, but Vida stopped her. "No. Go change. You can't look like a goth cowgirl. Let's get something nicer."

There was nothing in Carolina's chest of drawers that matched Vida's definition of *nicer*, but Vida pulled another black shirt from the drawer and shook it to see the print. It read *Easily Distracted by Dogs and Horses*.

"Perfect," she muttered. She found a pair of less-worn-out jeans and handed them to Carolina. "Here," she said, handing her the new outfit with a satisfied expression on her face. "I'll turn around so you can change and tell me why you're acting so sad, cowgirl."

Carolina didn't like to do as she was told, except with Vida (and, nowadays, perhaps Kimber). When her friend turned around, she exhaled the heaviness that had been pressing down on her chest and said, "I don't even know where to start."

"At the beginning is a good option," Vida said. Her hair had green tips now. She looked like the promise of spring with green pastures, blue sky, and warm sun.

Carolina struggled with the zipper of her pants. There was a reason this pair didn't look so worn out, and it was because she usually wore the same pants until they were destroyed while the rest of her wardrobe seemed to shrink or she grew.

"It's just that . . . it's not like I'm jealous, you know? But I'm not the most skilled student in Paradise, for all my parents say to the contrary."

"And what else?"

Carolina tried to find two socks that matched, but since it looked like this miracle wouldn't happen, she just took two that had belonged to the same batch—a pink and a purple that at least had the same design of horseshoes. "I'm frustrated with Shadow, and honestly? With Pepino too. He could be a little more adventurous and go on a gallop every once in a while, don't you think?"

"Well, I'm not an expert on horses, but you've said that Pepino is obedient, and that he's older and he's never been fast, right?"

"Right," Carolina muttered.

It was unfair to ask him to do things beyond his skill level.

"And how about Gisella?" Vida asked, bringing up the one subject Carolina had been trying to avoid.

She was all dressed now, so she plopped on the bed. At the sound, Vida turned around, and without a word, she grabbed a brush from the desk and started braiding Carolina's hair.

"She's almost done with the program, you know? She's getting pretty good at her posting trot, the last of her requirements."

"And what's the problem?" Vida asked.

Carolina was glad her friend couldn't see how she was blushing as she confessed, "I don't think I made a good impression on her."

Vida didn't say anything right away, but then she added, "She didn't give up though. That has to count for something."

"But what if she gives us a bad review and we don't get the funding for more students, Vee? What are we going to do?"

Vida slipped a hair tie onto the finished braid and gently turned Carolina around. Her face was open and honest. "What are you really afraid of if that happens?"

Carolina's eyes prickled and she lowered her gaze. "If that happens it will mean that I failed. That I'm not a good teacher, you know? And then Unbridled Dreams will have to close, and those kids who would've had a chance to love horses won't—"

Carolina was on the verge of tears. She'd been so lonely lately, even though the barn was full of people. Besides the classes, she had the read-to-a-horse program. A record number of kids had shown up for last story time.

Unbridled Dreams seemed a success from the outside, but Carolina didn't feel like anything she had done had helped it succeed. In fact, she felt it succeeded in spite of her and not because of her.

Vida hugged her. The scent of her vanilla shampoo made Carolina's nose tickle, but most of all, it melted her fears.

"No matter what, you're not a failure. Is that clear?" Vida said. "Look at this puppy. You've turned him from fearful creature into a loving fluffball. And me into a fluffball lover, in spite of how much he sheds."

As if he were waiting for this cue, he pounced on the girls and covered them with kisses. He only stopped when Vida started sneezing.

"Thank you, Vee," Carolina said, looking down at her feet.

"Let's go down to the arena," replied Vida.

Carolina had never said no to these words, and she wasn't going to start now.

Boo tried to follow them out of the cottage, but in that moment, Bracken showed up.

"Your mom said I could come babysit Boo for a little while," he said, puffing out his chest at the big assignment he'd been given.

Carolina and Vida tried not to laugh until they were out of earshot of the little boy. They wouldn't want to hurt his feelings.

Carolina was glad she didn't have to make the trek to the big arena on her own. It was all different with a friend by her side.

She arrived just as Shadow and Gisella were completing the join-up.

Carolina's heart seized with jealousy when Shadow approached Gisella like a puppy. A giant, well-behaved puppy.

And then Shadow wrapped himself around Gisella in a way that made Carolina long for that connection with the gelding. She could almost feel the warmth of his hair on her cheek and the trust in his deep brown eyes that looked so much like hers. When Shadow lifted his head, he locked eyes with Carolina and tossed his mane to the side, and it seemed like he was mocking her.

She swallowed the knot in her throat.

Without even needing Kimber's help, Gisella got in the saddle and started directing Shadow through all their exercises perfectly. As Kimber called out instructions and pointers, Shadow walked in every direction Gisella commanded. He stopped and waited for her. They did figure eights around the barrels.

Everyone clapped, and soon, Carolina couldn't help becoming invested in what was happening. Shadow and Gisella were doing well, and that filled Carolina with pride. Even if she wasn't the one who'd taught them.

She was on the edge of her seat when Gisella switched from walking to trotting. She started posting right away.

But in that moment a streak of fur crossed through the arena.

"Was that Luna?" Vida asked.

Carolina was already on her feet.

Bracken dashed behind Boo, his cheeks **bright** red, his white-blond hair pointing in every direction. He stopped as if to catch his breath, a hand to his side as if he had a stitch.

"Boo!" he cried out. "Come here this minute!"

Boo looked over his shoulder and ran faster toward Shadow, who retreated a little. Carolina saw the look of horror passing over Gisella's face, but the younger girl didn't panic. She held on to the reins and looked straight at the dog, which in turn made Shadow feel more confident.

Carolina admired her in that moment for keeping her cool.

"Boo!" she called, in a way that hopefully told him he wasn't in trouble.

At the sound of her voice, he switched directions and ran toward her. Her shoulders fell with relief. She had him. But the little troublemaker ran right between her legs and darted back outside.

Bracken was on the verge of tears when he said, "I'm sorry. I think I didn't close the door properly, and he wanted to be with you. I'm so sorry."

"It's okay," Carolina said. She had to fix this. "I'll go get him."

She left, regretting that she wouldn't see the rest of Gisella's class.

The day should have been glorious. Everyone was celebrating Gisella, the first student, and Chelsie's accomplishments. But Carolina felt like a failure as she headed outside to look for her dog by herself.

17

Just Like a Dance

Carolina's first impulse was to ask her dad to come and get her dog. She couldn't do it though. She'd promised to train him by the time springtime came. Snow lingered in these northern latitudes, but spring was just around the corner. It would be at least a month until the songbirds ventured back into these parts and brought balmier weather with them, but green grass was already shooting from the sides of the gravel path.

At least the mud gave her a clue of where Boo had gone.

"Boo!" she called, trying to sound like she wasn't losing her patience.

She was almost at the beginning of the trail when she saw

Boo running through some bushes that had burned a few years ago and hadn't healed yet.

She darted toward him.

He ran and ran.

Carolina felt like crying. She'd never catch him now.

He didn't obey her at all.

Shadow didn't like her.

Gisella preferred Chelsie instead of her. If only she spoke better Spanish! If only she hadn't been so bossy!

She had never felt worse in her life.

The sound of footsteps crunching in the gravel startled her.

She turned around and saw the last person she expected to find: Gisella.

"Hey," Gisella said, touching her shoulder. "Don't be sad."

Her English was still improving, but now she sounded so much more confident than even a few weeks ago.

"I'm sorry I missed the rest of your class. You looked lovely," Carolina said in Spanish, sniffing back the tears that wanted to escape, just like Boo. "I wanted to see you . . ." She tried to find the right word in Spanish but gave up. "I wanted to see you posting."

Gisella shrugged. "I don't know the Spanish word for posting either. The other day I was trying to tell my mom about it, so we had to use Spanglish. Sometimes I forget words too, you know?"

"Really?" Carolina said, surprised.

Gisella smiled.

"From what I did see, you were doing great at posting. How did you get it so fast?"

"Well . . . One day I overheard you say that horses play a music depending on how fast they go."

"Their gait," Carolina said. She hadn't intended to correct Gisella, but some habits are hard to break.

"Exactly," Gisella said, unfazed. "And I realized that it is like a dance, you know?"

"Dancing with the horse?"

"I hope it's okay that I mix two things I love: dancing and riding."

Here she had been trying to teach Gisella her way of doing

things, when the truth was that it didn't matter how one got to a solution as long they got good results. How many times had Papi told her that? Her stubborn head had to hear it a different way, she supposed.

"What are you doing here?" she asked. "Your lesson can't be over yet."

Gisella shrugged. "I wanted to help you. Kimber said I could take a break and go back once we found Boo."

"I did what I saw you do with Boo, calling him with a sweet voice, but it's not working this time."

Gisella's cheeks blushed bright red. "Instead of either chasing Boo or just waiting for him to come back whenever he feels like it, why don't you meet him halfway?"

It was like Gisella flicked on a lightbulb in Carolina's mind.

She had read up on horse training, trying to find the right thing to do with Shadow. Trying to figure out if what the trainers on YouTube said was right, or if what Kimber said was right. But she hadn't looked for what would work for her and Shadow as a pair. After all, they had to work together instead of pulling in different directions. And maybe if she stopped long enough to listen to her own instinct, she'd find the missing puzzle piece.

"Okay," Carolina said. "Do you want to come with me?"

Gisella nodded, a blazing smile on her face. "I thought you'd never ask!"

They were both connected with one purpose: finding Boo.

They walked in silence for a few minutes, and then Carolina asked, "If you were scared of horses, why did you sign up for lessons?"

Gisella laughed nervously. "Actually . . . my mom wrote the application for me."

Carolina gasped. "What?"

"Listen, I'm sorry, okay? I hope I don't get in trouble, but I was scared of horses because I was scared to try something new."

Carolina had so many questions, but she realized Gisella had a lot to say too. And this time, instead of filling the silence with her own voice, she yielded an invisible microphone to Gisella. She waited until Gisella took a big breath and kept going.

"Tessa told me about the program, but I was nervous I

wouldn't fit in. But Chelsie was so friendly . . ." She looked away as if she couldn't meet Carolina's eye for fear of offending her. "And the truth is, once I saw you riding, I wanted to be just like you. Especially after that day you fell off Shadow. You still got on even though it must have hurt. I would've been terrified to try again, but you got back in the saddle."

Now it was Carolina's cheeks burning. "Just for a walk."

"Still," Gisella said. "That taught me that it's okay to fall as long as you try again. You helped me try even though I was scared. Thank you."

Carolina was speechless. All this time, she had thought she wasn't teaching Gisella anything worthwhile. It turned out actions speak louder than words. They even translate better across languages.

Carolina was glad they had a chance to talk, away from the others, away from the stables. She was glad Gisella had seen things Carolina couldn't say aloud or even with words.

"There he is!" Gisella said, pointing ahead.

Boo was perched on a big slab of rock that jutted out of the foot of the mountain.

Carolina called him, and his ears perked. He looked in her direction, as if he were smiling.

"Boo, come!" she said.

Boo stared at Carolina, as if daring her to either chase him or call him again. She took a slow step toward him, trying to control her breath so she'd send him cool vibes. And then she blinked and didn't see Boo at the rock anymore.

Her heart fell.

"Oh, Boo," she said, thinking he'd run off ahead on the trail.

But right when she had lost all hope, she saw a whirlwind like a dirt devil dashing in her direction.

"He's coming!" Gisella said.

Carolina took another step toward him.

Boo reached them and barked once, as if saying, "Here I am!" And he sat, waiting for directions.

"That's a good boy," Carolina said, crouching to ruffle his hair.

Boo looked a little confused at first, but then he put a paw up. She didn't have any treats in her pocket, and neither did Gisella by the look of her turned-out pockets.

"If you want a treat, lead the way home." She pointed toward the little barn. They were too far to see it from here.

Boo barked once, and together, the two girls and the dog headed back home.

18

Let Me Try Something

That evening, Carolina and Chelsie met at the barn to say good night to Velvet even though they'd spent the afternoon together. After Gisella finished her lesson, the three girls had shared cupcakes and had a great time in which absolutely nothing dramatic happened, and Caro hadn't put her foot in her mouth.

Carolina asked, "Do you think Kimber is still at the stable? Is it too late to try something with Shadow?"

She'd been hesitating because she had no clue if her idea would work, but she had to do it or she wouldn't sleep a wink.

Chelsie knew her so well that instead of asking for details or talking her out of it, she said, "Let's go see!"

They headed to the big barn, and luckily, Kimber was still there, sitting on a tack box in front of Shadow's stall as if she were trying to solve a difficult math equation.

She was surprised to see the girls. "What are you two up to? Not trying to sneak a ride by yourselves, are you?"

Carolina shivered as she remembered all the trouble she and Chelsie had gotten into last year for taking things into their own hands.

"No," she said. "We've learned our lesson. Actually, we were hoping to find you here. I want to try something with Shadow."

Kimber rolled her eyes. "Now? I'm ready to turn in! It's late, and besides . . ."

But her words trailed off when she saw the disappointed expressions on the girls' faces.

"Okay," she said with an intrigued smile. "What did you have in mind?"

Carolina shrugged. "I'm not really sure. I feel like Shadow is trying to tell me something, and I need to figure it out. Like you said, horses don't have it in them to be stubborn. So why is he acting up only when I ask him to canter?"

Kimber thought and shook her head.

"It seemed like a different issue every time you two had a showdown. What do you want to try?"

"I want to try a join-up," she said, surprising even herself.

"But you both always end up frustrated," Chelsie said.

"I know," Carolina replied. "I want to try again. I want to help him, you know? After all, that's the first B. Be the leader your horse needs. A leader teaches, but sometimes, they learn from their students. All this time, I've been trying to get Shadow to listen to me. Well, that's not the problem."

"He can obviously hear you," Chelsie said, pointing toward him with her head.

"Now let's see if I can hear him," Carolina said.

In response, Shadow tossed his mane aside. Kimber was already getting a lead rope to try Carolina's experiment.

· U ·

It was still cold out, so they headed to the indoor arena. It was so pleasantly quiet. Carolina didn't think their problem was that there were too many distractions, but she was still glad the place was calm so she could hear what Shadow wanted to say.

Kimber and Chelsie stood on the edge of the arena and watched attentively as Carolina got Shadow in position to lunge in a wide circle around her.

"Walk," Carolina said, pointing her lunge line and body to the right.

He took off at once, walking as if he had places to get to.

She followed him around the turn, and when she stepped ahead, he changed direction without hesitation.

So far, so good.

They did a couple more transitions, and when she knew he was paying attention to what she was going to do next, she clicked her tongue and he started trotting.

They went over the same sequence of changing directions a couple of times. Then she clicked her tongue again, and he started cantering.

Like usual, he *looked* fine, but there was a break in his rhythm that jarred Carolina's ears. She had him change directions a few times, and Shadow obeyed, but he'd slow down and then speed up again. Unbalanced.

What is it? she wondered.

She closed her eyes and tried to visualize him. And then she understood. His left hind leg didn't pound as hard on the ground as his other three legs. Her heart sped up in excitement, but she listened for a few more beats.

"Whoa," she said, and he calmly came to a halt.

She waited in the middle of the arena, avoiding looking straight into his eyes. She wanted to give him space, but at the same time, she wanted him to step in her direction so she could make sure she was right.

But Shadow didn't budge.

And then she remembered what Gisella had taught her. About coming halfway.

Carolina wanted Shadow to know she was his leader, but most importantly, that they were friends. Or that she wanted to be.

She took a step forward, and he took a step back.

She was the one not budging now, but in a different way

from before. This time, she wouldn't give up on him just because he wanted to do things on his terms.

Slowly, she took another step toward him. He walked back all the way to the wall.

"Shh," she said in that voice she used with Boo. "I just want to see if you're hurt."

And maybe Shadow heard the love in her voice, and that she wasn't going to give up yet. Or he was tired of hurting. But he huffed out a breath, and he stepped toward her too.

She held her breath and took another step toward him. This time, he didn't step back. They both walked toward each other until they were nose to nose, breathing each other in.

She closed her eyes and almost melted when she felt the softness of his nose against her forehead. And then he wrapped around her in a hug.

She patted him lovingly. "You're such a good, good boy." She relished the moment. And then she turned and walked toward Kimber and Chelsie, who were silently jumping in place and high-fiving each other.

Shadow followed her, and Carolina knew her face would hurt the next day from all the smiling.

"You did it!" Chelsie exclaimed.

"I did! I think I know what the problem is," Carolina said.

"What is it?" Kimber asked.

"It's his left hind leg. I think it's hurt. Can you check?"

Kimber didn't waste time asking her how she knew. She walked to Shadow's leg and ran her hand carefully up and down.

"Oh my goodness," Kimber said, as if trying to keep the shock out of her voice. "His hock is swollen. I hadn't noticed before. It's not that bad, but it must be bothering him enough that he's cross-cantering."

Carolina felt a rush of relief. She had figured it out!

"What are hocks?" Chelsie asked.

"Their hind knees, the ones that point backward. Right, Kimber?"

Kimber kept inspecting Shadow, and said, "Yes, it's the link between the upper and lower leg, a whole system of joints, bones, and ligaments."

Chelsie and Carolina exchanged a worried look.

"Walking and trotting wouldn't bother him, but cantering does, which is why it only happened with you. You're the only one skilled enough to go on a canter or faster with him." Kimber straightened and gave Shadow a pat on the haunch. "I'll call Dr. Rooney first thing tomorrow morning. The treatment isn't complicated. Should be just anti-inflammatories and rest. Good job, Caro!"

Being complimented by Kimber and Chelsie was wonderful, but the best was the connection she had with Shadow.

He looked at her as if to say, *It took you long enough!*

She was impulsive and stubborn, but she was learning how to listen beyond what words said, and she felt like she had climbed to the top of the world.

19

We're All Works in Progress

A week later, after some well-earned rest and an injection of anti-inflammatories, Shadow was finally starting to feel better. And it showed. He seemed like a different horse. He was still very much a cabeza dura, but he didn't fight Carolina at all as she patiently walked him around the arena. Under other circumstances, she would've been impatient that she couldn't even ride him. But now that she and Shadow were starting to understand each other better, she loved the quiet companionship as they learned to become friends without words.

It's true that horses don't hold grudges. Carolina was learning more and more from him every day.

Chelsie, Gisella, and Kimber sat on their horses in the center of the arena.

They cheered when Carolina and Shadow arrived in a slow walk. She stopped him by Velvet, and the two horses touched noses in a hello.

"Good job," Kimber said.

She had done it. She had listened to Shadow. They were truly a team.

She had imagined this same outcome so many times, but a different way to get here. In the end, the result was all that mattered, not the way she'd arrived.

After she'd taken Shadow back to his stall, Carolina returned to the arena for Gisella's last lesson. She watched Unbridled Dreams's first sponsored student with bated breath, not because she was nervous, but because Gisella's form was textbook level! She and Leilani were a wonderful team. They looked perfect together as Gisella showed off a posting trot. Carolina leaned against Velvet's shoulder, Chelsie's leg just behind her, as they watched from the edge of the arena. Chelsie's eyes glittered with pride too.

"You're doing awesome, Gi!" Tessa hollered.

Gisella's parents clapped and cheered.

Chelsie leaned over to whisper to Carolina. "Student number one has been a success, don't you think?"

Carolina nodded. She probably wouldn't get to read the letter Gisella had sent to the donor, but in Carolina's mind the first step of experiment Unbridled Dreams had been a thundering success.

It hadn't been easy. But nothing worthwhile ever was.

Well, except loving Boo. He'd grown in the last few weeks, and now sat with his hip against Carolina's foot, panting with a doggy smile on his face. He was the loveliest dog that had ever existed in this world. Not perfect, but as her mom liked to remind Carolina, we are all works in progress.

· U ·

Later, when the students and visitors had left Paradise Ranch, Carolina was finishing her evening chores. Boo heeled her at all times, and Luna watched from the rafters. The two of them, dog and cat, still had to make their peace, but for now, they respected each other's space.

Suddenly, Carolina heard a whooping sound from the mansion.

She peeped out of the barn to see what was happening, and Chelsie came running to her, a paper flapping in the wind.

"We got it! We got it!" she chanted.

Carolina's heart went into full-on gallop mode.

Chelsie reached her and the scent of her strawberry lip gloss reminded Carolina that spring was in the air.

"Caro, look at this!" Chelsie said.

Boo had no idea what the girls were saying, but he jumped up and down, bouncing on his hind legs like a circus dog. At the sight of him, the two girls burst into laughter.

"Read it!" Chelsie said, wiping her eyes. A little bit of black mascara smudged on her eyelid, and Carolina wiped it off for her friend and then looked at her with a question in her eyes.

"Oh, shush!" Chelsie said. "It was in the thank-you present Gisella's mom left me today. I wanted to try it right away."

A thank-you present? Carolina tried not to indulge the familiar stab of jealousy that she felt.

Gisella had no obligation to give her a present too. After all, they were friendly now, but not best friends. And Chelsie had been Gisella's official mentor.

Carolina grabbed the paper from Chelsie and read.

It was a printout of an email.

"The donor! The apparel company!"

"Read it!"

Carolina's eyes scanned the paper, but then emotion made the letters blur and swim. The donors had written to them and copied in Gisella's letter for them to see.

"I can't!" she said, not able to believe the wonderful things Gisella had said about Unbridled Dreams.

"Here," Chelsie said softly, always ready to help.

She cleared her throat and read, "'I didn't want to give Paradise a chance. I was scared and angry that I had to move from Florida. I was scared of horses. I wasn't sure I would ever learn to love them. But seeing how the girls commanded the horses with so much confidence made me want to try to be like them. Especially Chelsie. She was patient and funny. She befriended me even before I ever applied for the program. And Carolina was fantastic. I remember the day she fell from Shadow, a spirited Arabian. Now, don't think this was something dangerous. She was wearing a helmet and had followed all the safety protocols. But there's a saying at the little barn that if you haven't fallen from a horse, it's only because you haven't ridden enough. Carolina fell, but she dusted off her pants and up she went again. Carolina was the one to suggest I rode Shadow. At first, I was scared, but he was perfect. I needed an experienced and decisive horse since I'm still shy around them. But Carolina does not need to borrow the strength from a horse. She has it inside her. I was there when she finally achieved her goal. I almost cried with how beautiful the sight of her and Shadow was. And I wanted to be more like her. She was a great teacher even when she wasn't telling me what to do. She also knows how to listen, which is the perfect example of being a good leader.

"'Now, I'll volunteer in any way to earn more riding lessons because I have definitely been bitten by the horse-riding bug. Thank you for making this possible for me. Without your help, I would not have been able to participate of this program because my family couldn't afford it. I wish more children could experience what I did these last twelve weeks. With friends like these, I finally feel at home. Thank you!'"

Carolina didn't know what to say.

"There's more," Chelsie said, her eyes beaming. And Carolina could tell that as wonderful as the letter had been, the part Chelsie had been celebrating was coming next. She braced herself.

"'. . . and this is why our company is pledging to sponsor two more children to do the twelve-week program. Also, we will continue supporting Gisella. Not that we want her to fall off a horse, but we were touched by her enthusiasm at learning a new skill, and we don't want her to lose the progress that she has made so far.'"

The two friends were crying and laughing as they jumped in place. Boo sat obediently next to them, and the horses spied from the stalls, Twinkletoes's happy bray joining the sound of the girls' joy.

20

Next!

The news that they would be able to bring more students into the program had quickly spread over the surrounding area, and every day applications flooded into Paradise Ranch.

They arrived in email. In the website form. And also through the flyers that Carolina's mom had placed at the library and at school and the ones that Heather had taken to town.

Reading the applications was a lot of work, and some nights Carolina stayed up, a little overwhelmed by how many children needed the healing power of horses.

Unbridled Dreams was new, but it was becoming a community for those who had been excluded from the world of horses for too long. Most students paid for the classes out of pocket. Carolina and Chelsie had talked about how this didn't necessarily mean that the family could afford it. It might mean a lot of sacrifice for their child to have this opportunity. And so they treated each payment and new student like they were sacred, because they were.

Kimber and the girls had vowed that they'd squeeze every bit of juice out of every lesson so that the kids could enjoy their time as much as possible. Because it couldn't all be learning. Often, the most change and progress happened thanks to friends and fun.

For the last couple of nights, they'd been stuck between three candidates. They all sounded like they'd be perfect fits for the program.

"We need to decide tonight," Heather told them as she handed out homemade strawberry rhubarb tarts.

Carolina had noticed how even though the big house was more modern and had every luxury, at the end of a long day of work they all flocked to the cottage and its coziness. She wouldn't have it any other way.

She sat on the floor with a hat that held three names from

the most outstanding applications. Chelsie, Boo, and Bracken were there too.

Bracken was waiting for Loretta to be done with lessons. His reading had improved in leaps and bounds since he started coming over to the ranch to read to the animals. Even JC's new chickens would end up reciting books since they'd heard so many stories.

Papi, Andrew, and JC were working in the big barn, bedding down new horses that were arriving from a rescue ranch. Carolina couldn't wait to meet them. Papi had told her that among the newcomers was an old-fashioned Percheron. His name was Napoleon. She was excited to meet him because she didn't really have any experience with what people called cold-blooded, or draft, horses.

Now that the weather was warming up day by day, she was itching to take Shadow to the trails. She'd caught him looking at the mountains with longing, as if there was something on the other side that called only to him.

She was falling for him, which she knew was a bad idea. Shadow had an owner from town, and Kimber had mentioned that the family might move back to California. She didn't want to become too attached to the Arabian if he was going to leave her. She didn't think she could stand the heartbreak.

And their donor had agreed to sponsor two more students, but . . . what about after that? What would they do if the next kids didn't enjoy the program as much?

Carolina reminded herself to be present. She was here, on her favorite shaggy carpet that was old but beloved and comforting. She was in the warm kitchen with her friends—and Bracken, her little shadow. She didn't know what was coming next for Paradise, but she knew she'd be surrounded by support.

"Is Kimber not coming?" Carolina asked, trying to put off the moment of choosing the next person.

"She's still with Loretta," Bracken said. "And you know my sister won't interrupt her class or cut it short for all the gold in the world."

Yep. That was Loretta. She wanted to be perfect for her show. Well, she had to learn that perfection was the enemy of progress all by herself.

"Once the new trainers arrive," Mom said, "Kimber can have more breathing room."

"Speaking about other trainers, Tyler wrote to me asking if he can come for the summer break," Heather said offhandedly, but Carolina almost jumped with joy.

"Tyler is coming back?" she exclaimed happily. "Wait until you meet him! He's going to be the best vet one day, but for now, he's the best horse whisperer in the world."

"I'm ready for him to lend us a hand! I might not let him go back to school if he's as good as everyone says," Heather said.

Mom and Carolina knew Heather was joking, but still, Caro shook her head because there was no way Tyler would give up on college after having worked so hard to finally get his wish.

"Let's do this!" Bracken said, bouncing with anticipation.

"How are we going to pick?" asked Chelsie.

Following Kimber's precise instructions, Carolina said, "The three of us, Chelsie, Bracken, and I, will each get a slip of paper from the hat, and then Boo is going to help us pick."

At the sound of his name, Boo's ears perked up. He was

sleeping by the heater vent, but Carolina knew he was alert and paying attention to every word they said.

"We're going to have him sit and then we call him at the same time," Carolina said. "Let's see who he chooses."

She was confident Boo would come to her.

"Okay," Chelsie said, passing the three slips of paper carefully. "At the count of three."

They counted in unison. "One, two, three." They took a long breath and the three of them called, "Boo!"

Bracken's little voice sounded like a song. His cheeks were bright red with mischief. He kept his bright blue eyes on the ground and gripped his paper in his hand.

Boo took a couple of steps toward Carolina. She held her breath and willed him with her mind to continue. But when he almost reached her, Boo changed direction and bounded the last steps to Bracken and licked his face.

Carolina rolled her eyes at Boo, but she wasn't really annoyed. She was curious to see the name on the piece of paper Bracken held.

He opened it for everyone to see the writing.

"Rockwell Richards," Carolina read.

It was a boy. The first boy who would be part of their program.

"R and R," Chelsie said in a singsongy voice.

"R and R," Carolina repeated, excited.

Bracken's eyes were shining as he started to get up. "When my sister finds out the next student is a boy, she's going to be so excited! She's always complaining there are no cute boys at the ranch."

"Now, Bracken," Heather said through a chuckle, "you have to wait until we let him and his family know first. Okay? Let's not ruin their surprise."

Heather was so diplomatic. What she didn't mention was that once Loretta knew a new boy was coming to take lessons, the whole world would know about it.

They put all the applications away for next time. There would be a guaranteed student after Rockwell.

Carolina's heart was fluttering with anticipation. Maybe she and the new boy wouldn't become best friends. But she had lots to share . . . and to learn.

"Let's go say hi to the new horses," Chelsie said, and without more prodding, the three kids went flying down the driveway to welcome the newcomers, the latest team members of Unbridled Dreams.

Boo chased after them, and soon, he led the way, a trailblazer.

A couple of bald eagles circled above Paradise, and Carolina could almost taste the sweet scent of the green clover sprouting in the pastures.

Spring had finally arrived.

Acknowledgments

This book wouldn't have been possible without the patience, expertise, and guidance of my editor, Olivia Valcarce. Thank you for this dream come true. Thank you also to the Scholastic family: Aimee Friedman, Kelli Boyer, Victoria Velez, Mary Kate Garmire, Rachel Feld, and Jordin Streeter. Thanks to Stephanie Yang for the book design and Winona Nelson for the beautiful cover and illustrations.

Thanks also to Linda Camacho and the Gallt & Zacker team.

Also, thanks to April and Gary Cooper for letting me hang out at their barn with their horses and Bridle Up Hope for the inspiration. Thanks to Caitlin Gooch for all the work she does with Saddle Up and Read in bringing the power of horses to every child. (To learn more about this amazing program visit saddleupandread.org.)

Teachers, parents, and librarians, thank you for sharing my books with the young readers in your life. And thank you to all who choose to spend time at Paradise with Caro, Chelsie, and me. Reading is a superpower, and I'm so honored I get to write stories for you!

Like always, thanks to my family for the love and support.

See you on the range!

Here's a sneak peek at
Horse Country #3: Where There's Smoke!

Carolina's heart sputtered and sprinted. She recognized the first car as Loretta's mom's SUV. Loretta's lesson was after Rockwell's, but she liked to arrive early to spend time with Poseidon, her beautiful buckskin American quarter horse.

The gray car, though, could only be the new boy arriving.

She turned to her mom with a question blazing in her eyes.

Her mom, who knew her so well, smiled and nodded.

"Yay!" Carolina exclaimed.

She started to run outside, but her insecurities rose to the surface and stopped her in her tracks.

Now that Loretta was here, she'd surely be peeking into Rockwell's lesson—and judging. And what if Loretta made fun of her outfit? She wasn't fashionable like Chelsie or Vida, but she felt comfortable in her favorite outfit: jeans and a hoodie. Her jeans were new, but the hems were already smeared in mud. Her green sweatshirt, the one with the Unbridled Dreams logo her dad had created, had a couple of specks of dried dough. Her pink *and* purple ones were in the wash.

Or what if Loretta made fun of Carolina's unruly, long brown hair, like she always did? Trying to tame her hair was like attempting to rope a wild mustang with a length of ribbon: a waste of time. So Carolina had let it fall wild and free.

What if the new boy thought she was a mess?

"What's wrong, my love?"

Caro turned around to face her mom. Trying to keep her voice cheerful, she asked, "Do I look okay? Do you think I need to change?"

Her mom walked up to her and looked at her intently.

"You look like a perfect cowgirl." She wiped Caro's face with a paper towel. "What are you really worried about?"

Carolina bit her lip. "Do you think he'll like it here?"

What she meant to ask was *Do you think Rockwell will like me?* But lately, using the word "like" was a tricky business.

HORSE COUNTRY

Welcome to Paradise Ranch,
where everyone can get a second chance.

#1: Can't Be Tamed

#2: Friends Like These

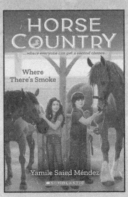

#3: Where There's Smoke